THE PANTS PROJECT

CAT CLARKE

Cover design and illustrations by Kristin Logsdon

Published by Sourcebooks Young Readers, an imprint of Sourcebooks Kids
P.O. Box 4410, Naperville, Illinois 60567-4410
(630) 961-3900
sourcebookskids.com

Library of Congress Cataloging-in-Publication data is on file with the publisher.

Source of Production: Versa Press, East Peoria, Illinois, United States
Date of Production: August 2019
Run Number: 5015978

Printed and bound in the United States of America.
VP 10 9 8 7 6 5 4 3 2 1

This book is dedicated to everyone who
tries to make the world a better place.

CHAPTER 1

"HAHAHAHAHAHAHAHAHA! You look *ridiculous*!"

Little brothers can always be counted on to reach peak levels of annoying at exactly the wrong moment. It must be part of their job description, and Enzo was really, really good at his job.

"Shut *up*," I snarled as I stomped into the kitchen and pulled out my chair so hard that it banged against the stove.

"Enzo! Apologize to Liv right now!" Mom glared at him until he muttered a halfhearted "sorry."

"Are you sure you don't want me to cook something? There's still time for me to rustle up something special for your big day." Mamma put her hands on my shoulders and leaned down to give me a kiss on the cheek.

"I'm not hungry." I knew that I had to eat—just a few bites to keep the moms happy—so I grabbed the tub of granola on the table and sprinkled enough to cover the bottom of my bowl.

Enzo wasn't even trying to keep a straight face. He was really enjoying this. I closed my eyes, but I could still hear him sniggering, just quietly enough to avoid being chewed out by the moms. I opened my eyes again and took a deep breath. I managed to pour milk into my cereal bowl instead of throwing the carton directly at Enzo's stupid face.

That was progress, right there. Except no one would ever know how hard I was working to keep my temper under control, because the whole point of keeping your temper under control is not doing things like throwing a milk carton in someone's face even though they clearly deserve it. Keeping your temper under control also means *not* punching people. That's the number one rule, apparently.

"Liiiv..." Mom said, stretching my name out to its breaking point, "Gram asked for a photo."

No. Way.

"It would mean a lot to her... I know you'd rather not, but the first day of middle school is a big deal, you know? Anyway, it's up to you."

Garibaldi chose that moment to put his big, slobbery head on my lap. It seemed as if he were trying to offer me moral support in my time of need. The more likely explanation is that he was just looking for a spot to wipe the excess drool from his mouth, but it made me feel a little better. At least *he* would never laugh at me, because (a) he's a dog and dogs can't laugh, and (b) if they *could* laugh, then all of the other dogs in the dog park would probably laugh at Gari for only having three legs, so he would totally understand how I felt.

I knew I could refuse to have my photo taken. The moms had always been cool about things like that, but Gram would be disappointed. *She* wouldn't understand.

"OK, let's get this over with." I got up and stood in the doorway while Mom snapped away on her phone. I couldn't bring myself to smile, and Mom knew better than to ask me to try.

"Done!" Mom came over and gave me a big hug. She whispered in my ear, "Thanks, sweetheart. I really appreciate it."

I shrugged and sat down again. I felt sick, and I must have looked sick because Mamma asked how I was feeling.

"Well...actually, I don't feel so good. Maybe... maybe I should stay home today."

Mom looked up from sorting through the photos on her phone. "Nice try, buster. There's no way you're missing your first day."

I knew when to give up. Mom has this weird sixth sense for when I'm faking being ill. It's as if she has laser eyes that can look right through my skin and actually see whether any viruses are festering away inside of me. Mamma's usually more sympathetic, but the two of them always back each other up. It's annoying.

I managed to choke down a couple of spoonfuls of soggy granola and half a glass of orange juice, just to keep the moms happy. Before I knew what was happening, breakfast was over. The clock was *tick-tick-tick*ing way too fast and it was time to go.

Mamma made me double-check my bag to make sure I had everything on the list. The new bag was just about the only good thing about this whole "going to middle school" business. The black-and-gray bag was leather, and it smelled really good when I stuck my head inside it. It reminded me of the first time we went for a ride in Gram's new car.

I had no doubt about the *worst* thing.

It was the thing I'd been worrying about all summer.

The thing that Enzo found so hilarious.

The thing that had made me throw a shoe at the mirror on the back of my bedroom door that morning.

The *skirt*.

I can't even begin to describe how wrong and awful it felt to put it on and pull up the little zipper at the side. A stupid, horrible, scratchy black skirt that came right down to my knees.

I'd stared at myself in the mirror, but my reflection

was all blurry from the tears in my eyes. They were angry tears. I wasn't sad; I was furious. It was so unfair. It suddenly hit me that I had to wear this stupid thing five days a week for the next three years.

How on earth was I going to manage *that*?

=

Bankridge Middle School had a strict uniform policy, unlike nearly every other school I could have attended. Everyone had to wear a white shirt, a tie, and a black V-neck sweater. I was fine with that. I actually kind of *liked* the idea of a tie (black-and-red striped). And the shoes were fine too—Mom had found these awesome black brogues online. But then whoever wrote the uniform policy decided (*whyyy?*) that girls had to wear skirts, while boys were allowed to wear pants.

Sexist. Dumb. Unfair. Even the moms agreed with me. Mom said she hadn't worn a skirt since her cousin's wedding back in the nineties.

I thought about trying to convince them to let me go

to another school, but Bankridge Middle School is the best school in the district. The moms are really big on education and how important it is and *blah blah blah.* Plus, Maisie was going to Bankridge, and there was no way I wanted to face the trauma of middle school without my best friend by my side.

So I was stuck with it.

"Girls must wear a black, pleated, knee-length skirt."

I bet I read those words a hundred times during summer vacation. I stared at the computer screen, willing them to morph into something sensible.

The problem wasn't the last word in that sentence. *Skirt* wasn't really the issue, not for me. The issue was the first word. *Girls.*

Here's the thing:

I may *seem* like a girl, but on the inside, I'm a boy.

CHAPTER 2

I realized there was something different about me when I was around seven or eight years old. I didn't just wake up one morning and think, "I'm a boy!" It sort of crept up on me and tapped me on the shoulder a few times before I started to pay attention. I began to think that the word "girl" didn't quite fit me. It was like a shoe that was too small—it pinched me.

It wasn't something I thought much about at first. It didn't seem to matter whether I was a boy or a girl. The moms treated Enzo and me exactly the same, except I was always allowed to go to bed later because I'm older. I was able to wear whatever I wanted at home *and* at school. Still, I knew it was something I should maybe talk to the moms about, but the words dried up in my mouth every time I tried. It's not really something you can just blurt out at the dinner table. *"Please can you pass the ketchup? Oh, and by the way, I think I'm a boy, not a girl."*

At first, I was just antsy when people used the word "girl" or "daughter" or "sister," or when they insisted on calling me Olivia even though I *told* them to call me Liv. Liv wasn't perfect, but it was a whole lot better than Olivia. Then I began to feel angry and upset for no reason. Except it wasn't for no reason. Most people would get angry if people insisted on calling them something they're not.

And then there was The Incident, which actually had nothing to do with me being a boy, but suddenly everyone was talking about my "anger issues" and watching me like a hawk all the time. So when it was time to go shopping for my school uniform, I didn't throw a tantrum. I just told Mom I would rather stay home, and she actually let me do that. She took my measurements and went by herself. It's a good thing too because I'd probably have Hulk-smashed the entire store.

=

The one thing I *was* excited about was my back-to-school haircut. It had become a ritual for the last day of summer vacation. The best part of the ritual was always the lunch afterward—I'd opted for noodles this year, after careful consideration—but the actual haircut itself was usually fun too.

Blake has cut my hair for as long as I can remember. She has a blue Mohawk and wears elaborate makeup that makes her look like she's in a sci-fi movie. She's super into comics too and even has tattoos of some of her favorite characters. I was dying to tell her about this new comic I'd been reading over the summer, so I wasn't exactly thrilled to turn up at the salon and find out that Blake was away on some last-minute yoga retreat.

Kitty was going to cut my hair instead. I'd never met her before. I try not to judge people by their appearance (for obvious reasons), but one look at Kitty told me we might not get along. I was ready to be proved wrong, and I asked her if she liked comics, just to check. She said no. I told myself it was going to be OK though. She had a nice, friendly smile and she offered me a cup of mint tea, just like Blake always does.

But then she sat me down in front of the mirror, narrowed her eyes, and said, "Right, what are we going to do with this?"

I didn't like the way she said "this." She didn't quite wrinkle her nose, but I could tell it was an effort for her not to.

I hadn't had a haircut since May, so my hair was a little bit too long, even for my liking. I asked for my usual cut. Super short at the back and sides and a bit longer on top. "Hmmm," she replied as she started tugging at the straggly bits of hair near my ears. "Have you thought about growing it out? I could tidy it up a bit for you in the meantime and before you know it, it'll be down to your shoulders."

"No!" I said a little too loudly. The woman in the

next chair stared at me in the mirror. I stared right back at her.

Kitty tried again. "I just wondered if you might want to think about something a little softer…a little more…"—You can just tell when someone's about to say something really annoying, can't you?—"…feminine."

I took a deep breath. "No, thank you. I'd like my usual cut please. With the clippers." I love it when Blake uses the clippers. It reminds me of that time the moms took Enzo and me to a farm and we watched the farmer shear a sheep.

"The clippers? No no no, I only use them for…" Boys. Men. But her words trailed off into nothingness when she saw the look on my face.

I looked around for Mamma, but she was sitting in the reception area talking on her phone. She was frowning a lot and speaking really fast in Italian, which obviously made me want to know who she was talking to. Mamma hadn't talked to her family in years.

I took another deep breath, just like Mom told me to do whenever I feel as if things are starting to get out of control. "Look, could you please just give me the haircut I asked for? Otherwise, I guess we'll have to make an appointment to see Blake after she gets back from her trip."

That seemed to do the trick. Kitty smiled too brightly and squeezed my shoulder. "OK, let me see what I can do."

To be fair, Kitty did a decent job in the end, even if it wasn't quite as short as I like it. She didn't use the clippers, but I decided not to say anything.

I could tell that Kitty wasn't too proud of her handiwork, but "the customer is always right." That's what the moms say about Monty's, the deli they've owned since before I was born.

That trip to the hair salon left me with a funny feeling, and not the good sort of funny feeling. The kind of feeling that makes you wonder what's wrong with you and what's wrong with other people, and why does everyone seem to have an opinion about things that have nothing to do with them?

Worst of all, I didn't even get my noodles. Mamma

seemed upset after her phone call and asked if it would be OK for us to have lunch at Monty's instead. She said she needed to speak to Mom. I didn't ask her what was up because I knew she'd tell me when she was ready.

"You're not too disappointed? About lunch?" Mamma asked as we waited in traffic.

"Nah, it's fine. I'm not really in the mood for noodles anyway."

That may have been a lie, but it felt like a good lie—the kind of lie that makes the other person happy.

There's nothing wrong with that, is there?

CHAPTER 3

The next day, Mom drove me to my new school even though it's only a ten-minute walk from our house. "Chauffeur service—for one day only!" she said. I took the opportunity to ask about Mamma's phone call yesterday, and Mom took the opportunity to shut me down completely. "It's nothing you need to worry about," she said.

"Mamma really hates her family, doesn't she?"

She smiled sadly. "She doesn't *hate* them. It's just… difficult, that's all. Anyway, are you feeling better about today? It might be fun, you know. New classes, new people…"

All I could do was stare at the skirt and the horrible, itchy tights. I'd thought the tights would make it better—that if I squinted my eyes, then I could almost imagine I was wearing skinny jeans. I was wrong. "It looks fine, Liv."

"It looks *stupid*."

Mom smiled sympathetically. "Why don't you give it a couple of weeks and see how you feel? I can always give the principal a call and set up a meeting if you're still not comfortable by then."

I just nodded, saying nothing. A couple of weeks would feel like a lifetime.

=

Maisie was waiting for me at the front gate, just as we'd planned. The uniform looked fine on her. It looked right. I caught her glancing down at my skirt, but she didn't say anything. It was the first time she'd seen me wear one, and we'd been friends forever.

People always seemed a little surprised that Maisie

and I were best friends. Teachers talked about how different we were, as if you had to be exactly the same as someone in order to be friends with them. The thing is, we weren't that different. Not really. We liked the same cartoons, the same books, and (mostly) the same movies. We liked the same flavors of ice cream *and* the same pizza toppings. The most important thing was that we found the same things funny (YouTube videos of dogs looking guilty, sneezing pandas, and people pretending to be dinosaurs).

I hadn't told Maisie my secret (or The Secret, as I'd started to think of it). There were lots of times when I nearly blurted out the words, especially recently. Over the summer, I'd spent a lot of time googling on the laptop (and then making sure to delete my search history, even though I was 99 percent sure the moms wouldn't know how to check it anyway).

I already knew the word. *Transgender*. I sort of liked it because it made me think of Transformers, and Enzo and I love those movies. "Trans" is the short version, which isn't quite as cool, but it is a lot faster to type. I found out that there are a lot of trans people out there. This one website had a bunch of their life stories, and I read them over and over again. Then I discovered more sites and blogs, and tons of videos on YouTube. It was just the best thing. I wasn't alone.

Sometimes I thought that Maisie would understand, and she would accept me for who I am. But looking at her that morning, in her skirt and shiny, pretty shoes with her long brown hair tied back with a matching black-and-red ponytail holder, I wasn't so sure.

She looked *comfortable*, whereas I felt about as comfortable as an octopus in a spacesuit. My shirt didn't seem to want to stay tucked in to the top of my skirt, and the itchy tights kept wrinkling at the knees. Tights are the worst invention in the entire world. After nuclear weapons and guns and things like that, obviously.

The one consolation was that my tie looked better than Maisie's. I'd practiced again and again until I got it just right. A bow tie would have been cooler, but they were *not* included in the dress code.

I could tell she was nervous too, but Maisie was just

better at being nervous than I was. I only knew because she was quieter than usual, and there was something tense and almost robotic about the way she walked—as if she'd forgotten how. Still, I was glad to have her next to me as we walked up the steps and through those huge wooden doors into Bankridge Middle School.

I took a deep breath and wished as hard as I could for the day to be over as soon as possible.

CHAPTER 4

Elementary school had been awesome. Now that I wasn't there anymore, it seemed even *more* awesome, and I realized maybe I should have appreciated it more at the time. There was no uniform, for starters, and there was a courtyard with a garden where we helped grow vegetables. The nice thing was that you knew almost everyone. Even if you didn't *know them* know them, at least you'd seen them around and recognized all of the faces.

Bankridge Middle School, however, had that *stupidly* strict uniform policy. There didn't seem to be any vegetable-growing whatsoever. Last but not least, the school was *huge*. The main building looked like something out of a horror movie—old and gray and menacing. Then there were some other newer buildings that looked as if they were clinging to it. They gave us all maps on orientation day, but I lost mine. I thought that I would never ever be able to find my way around it and get to my classes on time.

On orientation day, the principal told us that there are a little more than five hundred students at Bankridge. Five hundred! That's enough for an army or something. A very neat army with blazers and shiny black shoes. I think there were about 150 of us at my elementary school—a nice, sensible number. Enzo didn't know how lucky he was to have three more years there.

Maisie seemed to know where we were going. I teased her about having memorized the map, but she was too busy trying not to get knocked off her feet in the rush to class to even smile back at me. We stood back and plastered ourselves against the wall as a bunch of boys ran past, whooping and laughing and whacking each other with their backpacks. I watched them and wondered if I would ever feel comfortable enough here to do that. Or would I always be the one scurrying down the corridor, staying close to the walls, and trying to make myself as small as possible?

Everyone was so *tall*. It was weird to go from being the tallest, oldest ones at elementary school to being the smallest, youngest ones here. It was as if we'd progressed through all these levels on a video game only to find ourselves unceremoniously dumped right back at the start, and without any of the special powers we'd earned.

Luckily, Maisie and I had been put in the same homeroom. I was really happy about that. It was a big relief not to have to worry about who was going to sit next to me. It meant I could focus on all the other worries instead.

By the time Maisie and I walked into homeroom, I was feeling like maybe, just maybe, I'd be able to survive my first day. Then the homeroom teacher, Mrs. McCready, had to ruin everything with assigned seating.

Two people were to sit at each table: one boy and

one girl. Part of me wanted to say something—to tell Mrs. McCready that I should get to sit next to a girl, and there was no good reason why that girl shouldn't be Maisie. But something told me that wouldn't go down so well. Mrs. McCready looked a little bit like an angry eagle.

My table was diagonally opposite Maisie's. There was a boy already sitting in the seat next to the window. I'd always sat next to the window in school, so that was already annoying.

"Hi, I'm Liv. What's your name?"

The boy looked up at me, blinking slowly. He narrowed his eyes, acting as if I'd asked a really tough question. "Jacob. What kind of a name is Liv anyway?"

I disliked him immediately. He was obviously one of *those* boys. The popular ones. His dark brown hair was messy, but not properly messy. It was the kind of messy that requires a lot of time spent in front of the mirror and loads of hair gunk. He was slouched in his seat, perfectly at ease, like there was nowhere he would rather be. Whenever I sat that way at Gram's house, she always told me to "sit up properly—like a lady." You can probably guess how much I enjoyed that.

The only thing that gave me a glimmer of hope about Jacob was his eyes. They didn't seem to be the eyes of a terrible person. There was a kindness lurking there under the smirk.

I sat down next to him and shoved his leg so it was under his half of the table. *Why do real boys always take up so much space?* I mentally kicked myself. I don't know when I'd started thinking of them as "real" boys. I knew it was wrong; I wasn't Pinocchio. I was as much a real boy as Jacob—even if no one else could see it yet.

"It's *my* kind of a name." I concentrated on getting my pencil case out and lining it up with the edge of the desk. Then I noticed that the stupid skirt had ridden up my legs so I had to wriggle a bit in my chair to pull it back down again. Was the simple act of *sitting down* going to be a major ordeal from now on? Or would I get used to it, in time? *No. I will* never *get used to this. Not ever.*

Jacob rummaged in his bag and swore when

something clattered onto the floor. I leaned over to see what he'd dropped, but his back blocked my view while he zipped up his bag. A couple of seconds later, he turned around, triumphantly brandishing his pencil case.

It was the same as mine, except his was old and punctured with compass holes and had been scrawled all over by various pens. Mine was brand-new, bought especially for today. Gram had bought me a pink one, but Mom had my back ("*You know full well Liv doesn't like pink!*"). Mom took me to the store the next day and I chose a new one that was black, white, and gray camouflage. It made me feel like an urban warrior. (An urban warrior armed to the hilt with pens, pencils, and a Tyrannosaurus rex ruler that I stole from Enzo.)

"Isn't that a bit too butch for you?" Jacob asked with a smile. How many times had I heard stupid comments like that? It was *so* dull.

"Isn't it a bit too butch for *you*?" I asked, giving him the full-on evil eye.

We stared at each other for a second or two, and I wondered if I was going to have to fight him. It wouldn't have been the first time. Then he laughed loudly and said, “Fair enough. Cool name, by the way.”

“Thanks,” I said. “I like your watch.”

Jacob spent the next five minutes telling me about every single feature on his diving watch. I was super jealous, obviously. I was happy, though, or as happy as you can be on your first day of middle school, wearing clothes that make you feel about as far away from yourself as it’s possible to get. My first impression of Jacob Arbuckle may not have been a good one, but it was looking like it might have been wrong. Normally I hate being wrong, but I didn’t mind so much in this case.

CHAPTER 5

"Oh my gosh, you are *so* lucky!" Maisie grabbed my arm and dragged me out of the classroom.

My head was still reeling from the realization that math was going to be (a lot) harder than before.

"What are you talking about?"

She looked at me as if I were being particularly stupid. "That boy! Jacob Whatshisname! He is sooo…"

"So *what*?"

"Hot!" She elbowed me and said, "Don't tell me you haven't noticed!"

I sighed. "Hot" was Maisie's new favorite word. She'd started using it over the summer and it was already beginning to annoy me. She usually used it in relation to dumb-looking boys in bands, or actors in these terrible romantic comedies she'd started watching. This was the first time I'd heard her say it about a real person.

"I can't believe I'm stuck next to nerdy Nicholas Barker and you get to sit next to *him*!" Maisie's outrage made me laugh.

Someone behind us interrupted. "As if you would ever have a chance with Jake!"

We turned around to find two blond girls who'd obviously been eavesdropping on our conversation. I'd noticed them in the classroom earlier—*everyone* had noticed them. They were loud and obnoxious and already acting as if they owned the place. When Mrs. McCready had taken the roll, I'd listened for their names and learned that they were Jade Evans and Chelsea Farrow.

"Hi," Maisie stammered, "I'm Maisie and this is..."

"Yeah, whatever. We know who you are," said Jade, the blonder, taller one of the two.

"Sorry, I was just..." Maisie was blushing fiercely.

I was embarrassed for her, backing down in front

of these girls. Maisie always hated confrontation, so I stepped forward. "Thanks for the input, but this is a *private* conversation. And anyway, it's a free country and Maisie can say *what* she likes about *who* she likes."

I linked my arm in Maisie's and propelled her away from the two girls. "You can thank me later," I muttered under my breath.

She wriggled away from me. "We're supposed to be making new friends, *remember*?"

I was genuinely puzzled. "Why would you want to be friends with those two? They're awful!"

Maisie sighed. "How do you know they're awful? Why can't you give people a chance!"

I opened my mouth to speak and then clamped it shut again. How could I explain that sometimes you can just *tell* what people are like? You don't have to get to know them first. Sometimes it's best to judge them before they judge you. To dislike them before they dislike you.

Maisie rolled her eyes. "Forget it. I'm going to the bathroom. I'll see you in history." She walked away.

I was left standing in the corridor. Abandoned.

I needed to go to the bathroom as well, but there was no way I was going to follow Maisie. I'd just have to hold on until lunchtime. I was not looking forward to braving the girls' bathroom.

My first day was *not* going well.

=

By the time the bell rang at three thirty that afternoon, I was thoroughly fed up, but I managed to plaster a smile onto my face before getting into Mom's car.

She wanted to know *everything*. By the time we'd arrived at Monty's, I was exhausted from pretending that my day had been fine. Of course, then I had to go through it all again with Mamma and Dante while Mom went to pick up Enzo from karate. I was just desperate to get home and change into normal clothes.

Dante didn't comment on the skirt, but he did ask a bunch of questions about my day, and I actually started to feel a little better. Monty's is probably my favorite place in the world, and Dante is a big part of that. Mom says he's the best barista in town. I don't know about coffee, but he makes a killer hot chocolate.

I leaned against the counter while Mamma sliced some ham for us to take home for dinner. She let me have a sneaky slice or two (OK, *three*), which was just as well because I was starving. I'd barely eaten a thing at lunchtime.

When I was at lunch, I couldn't make up my mind whether the cafeteria was more like a zoo or a prison. Either way, it was somewhere I didn't want to be. Everyone seemed to know each other already—even the sixth graders. Jade Evans and Chelsea Farrow were sitting in the middle of a very busy table.

Maisie and I stood there with our trays, trying to figure out where to sit. I'd been worried she wouldn't want to have lunch with me after what had happened earlier, but she'd waited for me outside of class. "You have no idea where the cafeteria is, do you?"

I shook my head, feeling sheepish.

Another sigh from Maisie, but it was more like the

kind of sigh you aim at someone you actually like. She even smiled. "Come on."

Now Jacob was sitting at a table with a bunch of boys. They were laughing and joking as if they'd known each other forever. Maybe they'd been to the same elementary school?

I spied a table on the other side of the room and pointed it out to Maisie. A girl from our homeroom, Marion Something-or-Other, was sitting by herself, looking up hopefully every time someone walked past her table.

Maisie shook her head. "How about that one?" She nodded toward a table next to the one with Jade and Chelsea. There were only two empty seats.

I knew she was testing me, waiting to see what I would do. So I said, "Fine," and marched across to the table and sat down.

It was miserable. Maisie struck up a conversation with the girl sitting on the other side of her. The girl across from me was busy talking to the person sitting on the other side of her, so I was left looking at my lunch: a big globby pile of mashed potatoes and two grayish sausages. I squirted ketchup all over the mashed potatoes and mixed it altogether until it turned pink. I usually don't play with my food—I leave that to Enzo these days—but these were special circumstances. I stuck the sausages into the pink mash and sort of molded the whole pile so that it looked like Loki's helmet.

Maisie glanced over, saw what I was doing, and kicked me under the table. "*Ow!* What was that for?"

She just glared at me and turned back to talk to the other girl. I didn't even know her name because Maisie hadn't bothered to introduce me.

I felt sick. Lonely too. I ended up eating three bites of mashed potatoes and half a sausage, but by that time, everything was cold and even more unappealing.

The rest of the afternoon wasn't much better. I sat next to Jacob in Spanish, but he barely talked to me. He was too busy drawing something in the back of his notebook. I kept leaning over to try to see what it was, but his elbow was curled around the page, blocking my view.

I rushed out as soon as the bell rang, not even bothering to say bye to Maisie. I was worried that we'd just end up having another argument. Better to say nothing and start fresh tomorrow.

CHAPTER 6

The next couple of days weren't much better. Friday afternoon couldn't come soon enough. I'd been lectured (twice) about my shirt not being tucked into the waistband of my skirt and (once) because my shoelaces were undone. I'd gotten holes in my tights (twice)—those things are more fragile than a butterfly's wings. And, worst of all, the skirt continued to be a skirt, which was about the worst thing it could do, but not that surprising.

I tried talking to Maisie about it at recess on Wednesday.

"I really don't see the point of skirts now that pants have been invented."

"Some people like skirts, you know," said Maisie.

"Yeah, well some people are idiots." I winced. "Not you, obviously. I just…it's this stupid dress code."

"You knew there was a dress code before you came here."

This wasn't going so well. I'd expected Maisie to be sympathetic. That's kind of a best friend's *job,* isn't it?

"I hate it here." I kicked the wall to emphasize my point. So now, I was in a terrible mood *and* had a sore toe. *Good work, doofus.*

"It's just a skirt, Liv. Don't be such a drama queen."

There were probably worse things Maisie could have said right then, but that was right up there with them. Sometimes, instead of getting angry and shouty, I go quiet instead. This was one of those times.

I didn't say another word until Maisie apologized. It took approximately forty-seven seconds for that to happen. "I'm sorry. I know you hate skirts and dresses and girly stuff. But I don't. So I guess it's hard for me to understand…but I want to try."

It was the perfect opportunity to tell her the truth

about me, but the bell rang and our next class was on the other side of the building, so we had to rush. If I'm being entirely honest, I probably wouldn't have said anything, even if we hadn't been interrupted by the bell. I wasn't ready. Not even close.

=

Each afternoon, I changed out of my uniform and into jeans and a T-shirt the minute I got home. If the clothes didn't need washing, I stuffed them into the bottom drawer and slammed it shut.

Even after I'd changed into normal clothes, it still took about an hour or so to feel like *me* again. I also made sure to take off my watch and hide it in my bedside drawer. That way, I wouldn't have a constant reminder of how many hours it was until I had to get ready for school again. I had to be extra careful not to look at the time on my phone, and I studiously avoided glancing at the clock in the kitchen at mealtimes. It was hard work. Suddenly, time had become my enemy, and there was nothing I could do to fight it. It kept marching on, no matter what I did.

Only two good things happened in my first few days at Bankridge:

1. PE class. PE was pretty much the best thing about Bankridge because there were a ton of different sports. The only downside of PE was the locker room, but I'd already figured out how to deal with that. I ran the whole way to class so that I was the first one there and changed my clothes in record time. By the time everyone else trickled into the room, I was sitting there in shorts and a T-shirt, ready to go. At least the school wasn't stupid enough to insist that girls wear skirts for sports. The icing on the cake was that I won the 100-meter race in our first class. Jade Evans came second and was *not* happy about it.
2. Jacob eventually showed me the drawing he'd been working on, right before the bell rang on Thursday afternoon. It was a dragon with Mrs. McCready's face, complete with those weird,

old-fashioned glasses she wears. She was breathing fire, and if you looked closely, you could see numbers and math symbols in the flames. It was *amazing*.

Jacob acted embarrassed when I wouldn't shut up about how good the picture was, but I've always been terrible at drawing, so I guess that made me extra impressed. In the end, he just shrugged, tore the page out of the notebook, and said I could keep it. Before I could thank him, he'd bolted out of the room. I carefully folded the piece of paper and put it in my bag.

"What's that? A love letter to Jake?" asked Jade, bashing me with her bag as she passed my desk. "I don't think you're his type!" She walked away laughing, with Chelsea rushing to keep up. When she reached the door, she turned and shouted, "Nice haircut, by the way!"

I wouldn't have minded—Jade was easy to ignore, like a buzzing fly you can just tune out after a while—but I turned around and saw Maisie.

There was a smile on her face.

CHAPTER 7

On Thursday night, Mamma came into my bedroom and said there was something she wanted to talk to me about. I was hoping that she'd realized how unhappy I was at Bankridge, and that tomorrow she was going to march right into the school and tell the principal that the dress code was ridiculous. Instead, she told me that the phone call at the hair salon on Sunday had been from her brother Maurizio.

"But I thought you never talked to him?"

"I don't." I didn't have to ask why. Mamma's family doesn't approve of her being with Mom. They think she should have married some dude from her village in Italy.

Her dad said he never wanted to see her again, which is pretty much the worst thing a parent can say to their kid, if you ask me. I only know this because I overheard Mom talking to Dante about it.

"So why did he call you?"

Mamma reached for my hand. I couldn't tell whether it was to comfort me or her. "My father...he's very sick."

"How sick?"

"He's dying," she said simply. I was grateful she didn't try to sugarcoat it for me.

I squeezed her hand. "That sucks."

She snorted a surprised laugh. "Yeah, it does."

"Does Enzo know?"

Mamma shook her head. "I'll tell him in a minute." She took a deep, shaky breath. "Anyway, I just thought you should know. I should have told you sooner, but I... It was a lot to get my head around."

"Have you booked your flight?"

For the first time in the conversation, Mamma looked like she was about to cry. "No," she shook her head sadly. "I'm not going."

I didn't know what to say to that. Sometimes words are useless, so I hugged her instead. She said I shouldn't worry about her and that she would be OK.

After Mamma closed the door behind her, I lay on my bed thinking about this whole side of my family that I'd never met. I'd never even seen photos of them. It was hard to come to terms with the idea of this man even existing, let alone dying. It was impossible to think of him as my grandfather.

I was trying to work out whether I felt sad or not when my phone buzzed with an incoming message. It was Maisie—*finally*. I'd text messaged her as soon as I got back from school to ask why she'd smiled when Jade was mean to me.

I was smiling about something else.

What?

I can't remember. Why are you making a big deal about this? I'm sure Jade didn't mean anything by it. Anyway...did you see that new show they just put on Netflix? I've watched four eps already!

I had more important things to think about than TV shows. I didn't want to tell Maisie about Mamma's father though. It felt too private somehow.

I've been thinking about the school uniform.

Not this again! You need to get over it.

I can't!

Girls have to wear skirts. It's just the way things are. I'm not saying this to be mean...I'm only trying to help...you know that, right?

I didn't reply. I was too busy looking up the school's website to read that dress code just one more time.

I had an idea.

CHAPTER 8

On Friday, I went to school early. The moms seemed pleased. I guess they thought it was a sign that I was settling in at Bankridge after all.

My first stop was the girls' bathroom. I locked myself in a stall and opened up my bag. I had that tingly feeling in my stomach—the one when you can't tell if it's nerves or excitement.

I took out a pair of black twill pants, which were rolled up and stuffed right at the bottom in case either of the moms had decided to do a random bag search. Not that they would ever do something like that, but it pays to be paranoid when you have a plan like mine. Mamma had been quiet at breakfast. She didn't even say anything when Enzo slurped his cereal milk straight from bowl. I didn't want to bother her with all of this uniform stuff when she clearly had other things on her mind.

I kicked off my shoes (after putting some toilet paper on the floor to stand on in my socks, *obviously*) and put the pants on.

Marion Meltzer came into the bathroom when I was checking myself out in the mirror. When she saw me, she scurried right back out again. I guess I wasn't the only one too terrified to use the bathroom when there were other people in there.

After one last look in the mirror, I slung my bag over my shoulder and headed out into the corridor. Most people didn't even notice, which was disappointing.

Jacob was already there when I arrived in homeroom. His head was resting on the desk. I thought he might be asleep, but he raised his head when he heard me come in. He looked pale and kind of pinched.

"Are you OK?" I asked, dumping my bag on the table.

"Yeah," he said, vaguely. "Yeah, I'm fine."

"You don't *look* fine."

"Um...headache."

It was obvious that he was lying, but I didn't mind. I know what it's like to want to keep things private.

"Well? What do you think?" I put my hands on my hips and puffed out my chest in my very best superhero pose.

"What do I think about what?"

I waited until he noticed.

"Oh man, you are going to be in so much trouble."

I laughed, despite the tiny voice in my head saying that Jacob might be right. "They're really strict about the dress code, you know that, right? I heard that someone got suspended for three days for having their nose pierced."

I sat down next to him and smiled smugly. "Well, I'm not actually *breaking* the dress code, so I'd like to see them try to suspend me."

"What do you mean? I thought girls had to wear skirts."

"I am *wearing* a skirt. I just happen to be wearing

pants too. The uniform policy doesn't say anything about *that.*"

A slow smile spread across Jacob's face. "What are you? Some kind of evil genius?"

I shrugged nonchalantly, but inside I was buzzing with excitement. Sure, I was still wearing the skirt, but it didn't feel nearly as bad with the pants on underneath. I felt like some cool ancient warrior or something. I felt invincible.

=

Unfortunately, Mrs. McCready didn't think I was an evil genius or an ancient warrior. At least, she didn't say so when she sent me out of class after seeing my outfit.

She probably wouldn't have even noticed if Jade hadn't said, "I *love* your pants, Liv," in a sugar-sweet, extra-loud voice when I stood up to open the window. Of course, that made *everyone* look at me. I didn't mind. I wasn't stupid enough to think I was going to get through the whole day unchallenged. I just thought it might take more than ten minutes, that's all.

In the hallway, Mrs. McCready asked me to explain myself, so I did.

She shook her head and sighed. "I suppose you think this is funny, don't you?"

"No, ma'am." Jade and Chelsea were gawking at me through the tiny window in the classroom door.

"You know full well what the uniform policy means, even if the wording can be...*interpreted* differently. I could send you to the principal's office right now, you know." I winced. "But since we're not even through the first week yet, I think I could be persuaded to give you the benefit of the doubt, just this once...provided you go to the bathroom and change out of those pants this instant."

"Thank you, ma'am," I muttered.

"Now go. Quickly! Before I change my mind."

=

I arrived back just in time for the end of homeroom. Mrs. McCready nodded when she saw the skirt skimming my knees. Jade stared at me and whispered something to the boy next to her, which made him stare at me too. A few other people whispered and giggled. Maisie didn't even look up.

As we gathered our stuff when the bell rang, Jacob said, "It was worth a try. It's such a dumb rule."

I nodded, grateful to have someone finally agree with me.

Maisie must have sprinted as soon as she got into the corridor because by the time I got there, she was nowhere to be seen. *Weird.*

"I thought you looked cool," said a barely audible voice behind me.

I turned to see who it was, but Marion Meltzer was already hurrying away down the corridor, head down and books clutched to her chest. I didn't have a chance to say thanks.

I didn't manage to talk to Maisie until recess. It did not go well.

I tried to make a joke about the morning's drama, but she didn't respond. So then I asked if everything was

OK and she whirled around to face me. "What were you thinking? You know everyone thinks you're, like, a total weirdo now, right? Which means they think I'm a weirdo too—by association."

"Um…OK."

"What do you *mean* 'OK'? Don't you want people to like you?"

I shrugged. "I guess so…but why wouldn't they like me just because I wore a pair of pants? And how could it possibly affect how they feel about you?"

I thought those were perfectly valid questions; Maisie obviously did not.

"You're impossible sometimes. *Impossible*. I'll see you in class."

She stalked off, leaving me to munch my apple alone.

CHAPTER 9

On Saturday, Mamma took Enzo and me to the movies while Mom and Dante looked after the deli. The moms take turns working at Monty's every Saturday, and whoever isn't on duty takes care of Enzo and me. Mamma usually opts to go to the movies or a museum, and Mom usually takes us for a walk on the beach or a bike ride. Occasionally, Mamma will suggest we head to the beach on one of her Saturdays, "just to keep us on our toes."

Mamma's brother called again on Saturday night, but she closed the door to the kitchen so we couldn't listen to her conversation. Not that we'd have understood much of it. Despite Mamma's best efforts, my Italian is not good. *Il mio Italiano non è tanto buono.* So the three of us stayed on the sofa, and Mom turned up the volume on the TV. Enzo said he was feeling sad about Mamma's father, but he didn't know why because he'd never even met him.

"I think that's how we're all feeling, sweetheart. Just...if you guys could try to be on your best behavior while all of this is going on, I'd really appreciate it. I mean, you should be on your best behavior *all* the time, obviously. But I'm realistic enough to know that's not possible with you two troublemakers."

"Troublemakers? *Us*?" Enzo asked. He really has that wide-eyed innocence thing *down*.

=

Monty's is closed on Sundays, so we have one day a week when the four of us are all together. Usually, we pile onto the moms' ginormous bed and drink tea and eat hot buttered toast. Garibaldi joins in too, but I have to help him up because of his missing leg. Then we have to fiercely guard the plate of toast so that Gari doesn't gobble it up.

Sunday always used to be the best day of the week, but this Sunday was different. I woke up with this sick, heavy feeling in my tummy. The weekend was nearly over. That's how it felt, even though technically there was a whole day left.

I buttered the toast—right to the edges—and cut it into triangles, just like I always do. But it didn't feel the same. *Great. A whole day of the week* ruined *for the next three years.* The moms aren't stupid—they knew something was up. Mom gave me a big hug and told me that I was in charge for the day. Enzo wasn't too happy about that, but even his pouting face wasn't enough to make me smile. I told Mom that I wanted to stay home because I had homework to do. She agreed to that, but said I'd get to choose the movie for Sunday Movie Night and, more importantly, the snacks. "Nachos, fully loaded?" I asked, slyly. Maybe nachos would make everything better.

"Nachos it is!" she said with a smiling sort of grimace. Mom hates nachos, but the rest of us love them. Enzo and I always compete over how much cheese we can get Mamma to grate on top.

I settled down to start my homework after breakfast. Enzo was busy cleaning his room. That just shows you how much of a little weirdo he is—who on earth actually enjoys cleaning their room? Mind you, I think he just uses it as an excuse to line up all of his action figures "in order of awesomeness."

I finished the math problems in a few minutes. They weren't too hard, but Mrs. McCready had said we should expect them to be "more challenging" next week. I didn't like the sound of that, and I knew I needed to do well in her class, at least until she forgot about my little rebellion on Friday. We had twenty words of vocabulary to learn for Spanish, but I'd already done that during lunch on Friday while Maisie was busy chattering away to new people.

I left the biggest assignment until last. Our English teacher said he wanted to know more about us. He wanted us to learn all about each other and get to know each other better. We had to write a few paragraphs to introduce ourselves, talk about our likes and dislikes, and describe our families, as well as "something that's important to us." I've always enjoyed writing, though I prefer making stuff up *(Pirates! Monsters! Monsters who also happen to be pirates!)* over boring real-life stuff. But I actually got quite into this particular assignment. Mamma brought me a cup of tea, but I was so busy writing that I forgot to drink it.

I felt pretty pleased with myself when I read over my work. Oddly enough, writing it had made me feel much better about things. Maybe Bankridge wasn't *that* bad, and even if it was, almost everything else in my life was good.

CHAPTER 10

My cheesy feelings of positivity lasted until approximately 10:13 a.m. on Monday. The rest of Sunday had been OK in the end. Enzo and I had played "spies versus aliens" in the garden. I was the alien—I *always* had to be the alien. I didn't mind, because it meant that sometimes I got to kill Enzo by sucking his brains out with my special brain-sucking laser gun.

On Sunday night, I'd eaten a huge pile of nachos while we were watching *Indiana Jones and the Temple of Doom* (for the third time in three months). I went to bed feeling good about things. I was going to make more of an effort to settle in at Bankridge. I would even try to make new friends, if that's what Maisie really wanted. Most importantly, I was going to try to ignore the stupid skirt, or at least try not to think about it every three seconds. And if I *did* think about it, I would do my best to imagine that it was actually a kilt, and I was a brave Scottish warrior who would chop the head off anyone who dared to laugh at him.

On Monday morning, Jacob was in homeroom before me again. He said he'd spent the weekend helping his mom paint their bathroom. He just laughed when I pointed out the tiny, almost invisible flecks of paint on his face. "You should try washing, you know," I said.

"Washing? Hmm... I think I've heard of that. Tell me more!" he said with a grin, leaning back in his chair and linking his fingers behind his head.

"Well, you get some water, ideally hot water but cold will do, and then you get some soap or shower gel and you combine the two. It's like *magic*!"

We laughed a little bit too loudly, and Jade turned around to glare at me. Then she smiled at Jacob. I'm sure it wasn't easy to go from glaring to smiling in 0.2 seconds.

In English, Mr. Eccles bounced into the room with a little bit too much enthusiasm for a Monday morning. "Right," he clapped his hands together, "Let's get to know each other! I'll go first."

That was weird. None of us had expected *him* to do the homework too. It turned out he hadn't really done it; he just told us some things about himself. He was born in California. He's the youngest of three brothers. Everyone in his family calls him BB, which stands for Baby Bear. We all laughed at that, and laughed even harder when he said, "That's *Mr.* BB to you." He has two guinea pigs called Plink and Plonk and a fiancée named Amira. He told us that teaching is very important to him, and that he thinks it's the best job in the world. Somebody obviously forgot to tell him that video game tester is an actual real job that you can get paid to do.

We went in alphabetical order after that, and each one of us had to go up to the front of the classroom to read our essays. Jacob went first. I found out that his mom is really into feminism and teaches a course on it at the local college. His dad is a photographer for the local newspaper, and he has a sister named Chloe and a dog called Bob. He talked about the fact that he likes to draw.

When he was finished, he sat down next to me, and I whispered, "Your dog is called Bob?"

"Bob is an awesome name for a dog. You're just jealous."

I snorted a laugh and tried (unsuccessfully) to disguise it as a cough.

I listened as, one by one, my classmates talked about their lives. Jade said that "helping people less fortunate then herself" was very important to her. *Yeah, right.* Marion spoke so quietly no one could really hear her, but Mr. Eccles didn't say anything, which was kind of cool of him.

Maisie blushed her way through her turn. I could see the notebook shaking in her hands. She talked really fast and it was over before anyone had a chance to take in what she had actually said. She rushed back to her seat and sat down as quickly as possible.

It was my turn next. I took my notebook with me, but I'd memorized what I wanted to say. I talked about my dog and how one of my favorite things to do is take him to the beach. I glanced over at Jacob when I said Garibaldi's name, just to see the look on his face, and he was laughing. I accidentally looked over at Jade, who had her arms crossed and was trying her best to look bored.

I talked about Enzo and how he's a good brother most of the time. I talked about the deli and Dante, and about being allowed to sample the new cheeses.

"The thing that is most important to me is actually two things. Well, two *people*, actually. My moms. Even though they're really busy with the deli, and Mamma volunteers two nights a week, they always make time for Enzo and me. They always manage to make me smile when I'm feeling sad, or make me laugh when I'm feeling angry. And they didn't ground me for life when I thought it was a good idea to paint white stripes on Garibaldi to make him look like a zebra.

"My moms are the best parents ever, and I'm very

lucky to have them. I hope they think they're lucky to have me too."

There. I was done. I'd managed to remember everything I wanted to say without even having to look at my notebook once. Mr. Eccles had a huge smile on his face. "Thank you, Liv. That was wonderful."

That's when it happened. That's when I realized I'd made a terrible mistake. A voice piped up—a mean, spiteful voice. "You have *two* moms! *Ewww*."

A couple of people laughed as I made my way back to my seat. Mr. Eccles raised his voice and said, "Jade, get out of this classroom right this second!"

But it was too late. The damage was done.

CHAPTER 11

I sat down next to Jacob and stared at the desk in front of me. I stared really, really hard. Out of the corner of my eye, I saw Jade's shoes as she walked past my desk. As she went by, she whispered, "Gross."

"Out!" Mr. Eccles shouted.

I could feel people looking at me, and all I could think was: *Do. Not. Cry.* I don't think I've ever thought anything so hard in my life.

Mr. Eccles said that he wanted complete silence while he went out to deal with Jade. Of course, everyone started talking as soon as he left the room. I kept staring at the desk, wishing that time would speed up, or that time would stop for everyone else. If only I could hit the pause button and everyone would freeze, be stuck doing whatever they were doing (in the case of Wayne Garvey that would be picking his nose and eating it), then I could get up from my chair and slip out of the room, out of the school, and run all the way home.

Jacob was scribbling away next to me when Mr. Eccles came back in. Mr. Eccles said that he wanted everyone to know that what Jade had said was unacceptable, and that he'd sent her to the principal's office. He said that there are many different kinds of families, and that everyone should be grateful to me for sharing my experience with the group. I sank down lower into my chair. Why couldn't he just shut up? Why did he have to draw attention to me again? Everyone would forget all about it if he would just *shut up*.

He did stop talking eventually. People carried on, getting up and talking about themselves and what was important to them. One word seemed to pop up again and again. *Dad.*

Of course, I wasn't the only one without a dad. One

girl said that her dad had died four years ago. Kyle Walters said that he'd never known his dad, but he didn't seem particularly bothered about it. But even if they didn't live with them, the vast majority of people *had* dads. Of course they did. I knew that. It had been the same in elementary school, but for some reason it hadn't mattered then. No one had really cared, and those who had cared, like Maisie, were a little jealous. Not that their dads were terrible or anything, but there was something undeniably awesome about having double the moms.

I risked a glance back at Maisie, just to see a friendly face, but she looked away when our eyes met.

Just before the bell rang, Jacob pushed his notebook across the desk. It was another awesome drawing, and this one managed to make me laugh out loud, even though I was feeling terrible.

Jacob had drawn a picture of Jade as a supervillain, complete with pointy black mask and cape. The letters "MG" were emblazoned on the front of her outfit. A speech bubble emerged from her mouth: "The world will bow down to the power of Mean Girl! No one is as mean as I am. No one! MWAHAHAHAHA!"

"Can I keep it?" I whispered.

"To stick on the back of your bedroom door so you can throw darts at it?" Jacob asked, tearing out the picture and handing it to me.

When the bell rang and we were getting our things together, Jacob said, "She shouldn't have said those things. Jade, I mean."

I shrugged, trying to act like it was no big deal and I *hadn't* been trying not to cry for the past ten minutes. "It's fine. I don't care what she thinks."

He didn't actually have to say the words. The look on his face was enough to tell me that he wasn't buying it.

I packed up my bag as quickly as possible and said, "See you later."

I looked around for Maisie, but she was gone. My best friend was getting good at disappearing just when I needed her.

I spent all of recess outside. I walked around the entire school three times, picturing horrible things happening to Jade. Things like her hair turning into overcooked spaghetti. Or her having to walk barefoot over Legos everywhere she went.

I didn't cry, though. I was proud of myself for that.

=

I didn't get a chance to speak to Maisie until lunch-time. I'd managed to ignore the evil glares from Jade when she came back to class halfway through history class. I'd even managed to tune out the whispering. Even when you can't hear what they're saying, you can just tell when people are talking about you. It's like a sixth sense.

Maisie and I were in the lunch line, sliding our trays along the counter. None of the choices looked particularly appealing, but I went for lasagna in the end. (This turned out to be a *bad* decision. Mamma makes the best lasagna in the entire world; this one wouldn't even have made the top one thousand.)

"Are you OK?" Maisie asked quietly.

Finally. I was wondering when she was going to get around to asking.

I surprised myself with my answer: "Yeah." I hadn't meant to say that; the lie had just slipped out. I'd never really lied to her before about anything important. (And no, I didn't count keeping quiet about The Secret as a lie. That wasn't the same thing at all.)

I expected her to ask again because it should have been obvious that I wasn't telling the truth. But she didn't. She just said, "Good," and picked up a banana from the fruit bowl.

"I wouldn't stand too close to her if I were you, Maisie…it might be contagious." Jade, of course.

I turned to face her. She must have gone out of her way to walk past us because she wasn't carrying a tray. Chelsea was hovering next to her. "What might be contagious?" I asked with a fake polite smile on my face.

Jade didn't have a smile on *her* face. She narrowed her eyes. "You know what I'm talking about."

"No, I really don't."

Jade made this sort of disgusted *urgh* sound and flicked her hair over her shoulder. "Whatever."

I was aware of Maisie shuffling along in the line, leaving me alone to face Jade and Chelsea.

Jade leaned in close and hissed, "Don't think I'll forget about the trouble you got me in. Two detentions, all because of *you*."

I smiled a big, broad, *real* smile. "I'm very sorry to hear that." Jade looked as if she wanted to hit me, which made me smile even more.

She stuck out an elbow and flipped my tray over. The lasagna went *splat* on the floor. People laughed. Someone even clapped.

"Oh dear. How clumsy of you." Then she walked off before I could say or do anything.

I took a deep breath. *Stay cool. Do not go after her. Do not tackle her to the floor and shove her face in the mushed-up lasagna.*

The moms would kill me if I got into trouble. I'd been working so hard on my temper since The Incident. I gritted my teeth so hard that I thought they might shatter, fall out of my mouth, and land on the lasagna mush. Sort of like crumbly, extra-crunchy parmesan.

A lunch server came over with a mop and bucket to clean up the mess. I offered to help, but she shooed me away. I stepped back in line and another lunch server handed me a fresh plate of lasagna along with a sympathetic smile. They probably saw things like this happen all the time. Middle school was brutal.

By the time I sat down next to Maisie, most of the laughing and whispering had stopped. I chewed my way through the soggy, cheesy pasta, but it was hard to swallow. It felt as if a baby hedgehog were hibernating in my throat. I couldn't help thinking that if this was the way Jade was going to treat me just because I had two moms, how much worse would it be if she ever found out the truth about me? Something told me that Jade wouldn't exactly be understanding if she realized that I was trans. If she thought I was weird just because I wanted to wear pants, there's no way she'd be able to get her head around *that*. She'd probably say something stupid like I'm trans *because* I have two moms.

Maisie barely said a word to me during the rest of lunch. I could hardly believe that she was the same girl who'd defended me after The Incident. How could she have changed so much in just a few months?

CHAPTER 12

So. The Incident: the short version.

It was the last day of the semester. The last day *ever* of elementary school, and I ruined it by punching someone in the face. It didn't seem to matter to anyone that the punched person deserved it, even though Maisie did her best to explain. She told Miss Dylan and Mrs. Trewellyn that Danny Barber had been hounding her all day, teasing her about the fact that he wanted a "goodbye kiss." She told them that she'd done her best to avoid him and (repeatedly) told him to leave her alone, but he wouldn't give up. He lunged for her, lips puckered, at the end of lunch period. That's when I punched him.

I *had* to. That's what the moms didn't seem to understand when Mrs. Trewellyn called them in to take me home. "You never *have* to punch someone, Liv." That's what Mom said. "There are always better ways of dealing with these things."

She meant "talking," I guess, but talking wouldn't have stopped Danny Barber's big, fat, slobbering mouth from latching itself onto Maisie's.

Mrs. Trewellyn said that under normal circumstances, I would have been suspended for a couple of days. She said I should "count my lucky stars" that it was the last day of the semester. She told the moms that they should think about finding someone for me to talk to about my anger issues. It probably didn't help that I shouted "I DON'T HAVE ANGER ISSUES!" when she said that.

That night I overheard the moms talking about me. When I say "overheard," I really mean "eavesdropped on." They thought I was in bed, but there was no way I could sleep. I was *way* too angry to sleep.

"We should talk to her," Mom said.

"We *have* talked to her, Jax," replied Mamma.

"Not about the fight." I don't know why Mom called it a fight. That wasn't entirely accurate, was it? "She'll be going through puberty soon." *Puberty?* I grimaced. What did that have to do with anything?

Mamma sighed loudly. "We don't even know for sure… What if we're wrong?" Her voice cracked a bit then, like she was trying not to cry.

"Do you really think we're wrong?" Mom said, her voice softer and gentler than normal.

"I don't know what to think anymore." That's when Mamma really started crying. I wanted to hug her, tell her I was sorry, and that she didn't need to worry about me. I wouldn't punch anyone again. But I didn't want the moms to know that I'd been eavesdropping, so I crept upstairs and got back into bed.

It must have been about three o'clock in the morning when it hit me. I knew the reason they'd mentioned puberty. How could I have been so stupid? *They know. About The Secret, or at least, they think they know.* And just the thought of it—the suspicion of it—had been enough to make Mamma cry. That's when I decided that

I definitely had to keep quiet. I would do anything to *not* make Mamma cry.

=

Maisie had blamed herself for me being sent home from school, even though I told her that didn't make any sense. On the first day of summer vacation, she brought over some cupcakes that she'd baked especially for me. She'd iced each one with a letter so that they spelled "BEST FRIENDS" when you lined them up. Mamma let Maisie come in for a cup of tea, even though I was technically grounded.

Maisie thanked me for "rescuing" her. She giggled when she told me that Danny Barber looked really stupid with two cotton balls stuffed up his nostrils to stop the bleeding. She apologized for ruining my last day of elementary school.

The last thing my best friend said before she went home was that she would make it up to me. She *promised.*

Well, that wasn't such a short version after all, I guess.

Anyway, that's why I didn't do anything to Jade when she humiliated me in front of everyone in the cafeteria. Because I knew what would happen if I *did* do something: weekly counseling, anger management, difficult questions, and, worst of all, Mamma crying. Plus, it would have broken both of their hearts to find out that people were making fun of me for having two moms.

Anyway, the point is that Maisie had made a promise, and she'd just had the perfect opportunity to make it up to me, to tell Jade to leave me alone. That was all she had to do. I wasn't expecting her to punch anyone for me. Just do the right thing. But she had broken her promise. I couldn't help wondering if our friendship might be slightly broken too.

CHAPTER 13

My plan was to keep my head down and hope that Jade would forget all about it.

Things didn't quite work out that way.

Example: We were reading a book in English and Mr. Eccles asked a question about the father in the story. I put my hand up because, for once, I actually knew the answer.

I suppose it was inevitable that Jade would whisper, "What would *she* know about dads? She doesn't even have one."

Mr. Eccles didn't hear what she said, but he did hear the giggling and he glared in Jade's direction until it stopped.

Example: Someone had scrawled some horrible graffiti on my homeroom table. I don't even like to think about what it said. Let's just say it was hateful and mean and leave it at that. It didn't take a genius to figure out who'd done it, especially since she'd been there when I arrived, looking supremely pleased with herself. I chose not to react. I refused to give her the satisfaction. I just sat down and covered the word with my pencil case. I almost managed to forget about it until Jacob asked if he could borrow a ruler and reached for my pencil case before I could answer.

He put it right back down again, careful to put it in exactly the right spot. "Who did that?" he whispered.

"I'll give you three guesses, but you'll only need one," I whispered back.

His jaw tightened. "You should tell Mrs. McCready."

"No chance. It would just make things worse."

He sighed, but he didn't disagree. "Do you want me to talk to Jade?"

"May I refer you to my previous answer?" I said with a shaky half smile. It's the worst thing in the world when someone is nice to you when you're trying not to cry. At that point, it would have been easier to have Jade sitting next to me than Jacob.

"You know she's an idiot, don't you?" said Jacob. He turned around in his seat to glare at Jade. She didn't notice at first, but after a few seconds, she looked up and smiled. The smile slipped straight off her face when she saw how annoyed he looked. She glanced at me and then back at Jacob, putting two and two together (which was clearly not that easy for her since Jade is even worse at math than I am). Her cheeks flushed and she quickly looked away.

Jacob and I turned back around in our seats. I couldn't decide whether I was annoyed with him or happy that *he* was annoyed on my behalf. I was worried that Jade would think I'd told him that she'd been the one to write the graffiti. But when I really thought about it, things with Jade couldn't exactly get any worse.

=

It was going to be the party of the year. That's what everyone was saying. And I was most definitely *not* invited. Hardly surprising when you considered whose party it was: Chelsea Farrow's. Jade's BFF.

One other kid in our class definitely wasn't on the invite list: Marion Meltzer. I bet she didn't mind either since she hardly seemed like the partying type. People had started calling her Mousey Meltzer as soon as Jade came up with the idea. The lack of imagination it took to come up with that nickname was embarrassing, frankly.

A few days before the party, I was sitting with Maisie in the cafeteria when Chelsea and Jade strutted over to our table and stood behind us.

"So are you coming then?" Chelsea asked Maisie. She didn't even bother saying "hello" or "excuse me."

I'd been busy telling Maisie that this was the only middle school in the district that didn't allow girls to wear pants. I could tell that Maisie was only half-listening, swirling her yogurt with her spoon while she stared into space. The last thing she said before Chelsea and Jade arrived on the scene was, "But skirts are just *nicer*."

I would have been grateful for the interruption if it had come from anyone else—even a teacher scolding me about my shirt not being tucked in properly.

Maisie and I looked up at them. Chelsea repeated her question, louder this time.

"Um…" Maisie glanced over at me before looking at Chelsea and Jade.

"Well?" Jade crossed her arms. "We haven't got all day, you know. RSVPs were supposed to be in by Friday, just like it said at the bottom of the invitation in *big* letters. Chelsea's mom needs final numbers by the end of the day so she can tell the caterer."

Chelsea and Jade were acting as if I didn't exist, but there was something about the way they were doing it that was so fake and staged. It was obvious that this little scene was for my benefit. It had been at least four days since the last time they'd picked on me in the locker room after PE.

I turned back to my pudding, reminding myself for the hundredth time that it was best to ignore them. If there's one thing bullies hate more than anything, it's being ignored. They only want to get a reaction out of you. They can't *stand* it if you don't react. Of course, this is really, really hard to do. Particularly if you happen to have a bit of a temper.

"Er...yeah...I meant to..."

Jade sighed so hard I actually felt a whoosh of breath on the back of my head. "It's a simple question: Are you coming to the party or not?"

A few people were listening now, which was going to make it even more amazing when Maisie said no.

"Yes. I mean, yes, thank you. I'm looking forward to it."

What?

CHAPTER 14

Traitor. That was the word I used after Jade and Chelsea had swanned off from our table. They obviously didn't even care if Maisie went to the party.

Maisie didn't like being called a traitor. She doesn't have much of a temper; she tends to cry instead of getting angry. But not this time. Her eyes flashed and her mouth set in a thin, hard line. "It's not *my* fault you weren't invited."

Deep breath, Liv. Logic and reason. That's the way to go. "I'm not saying it's your fault. But can't you see what they're doing? They're trying to turn everyone against me."

"Not everything is about you, Liv."

"Then why did they invite everyone in our class except me? Oh, and Marion Meltzer, of course. Why would you want to go to the party anyway? Chelsea and Jade are horrible."

"They're *popular*."

"So? They're only popular because everyone's scared of them. Well, scared of Jade. Anyway, since when do you care about being popular?"

Maisie pushed her chair back quickly, scraping it against the floor. "Look, I'm sorry you weren't invited to the party. Maybe if you made more of an effort to fit in, people would like you a bit more."

"What do you mean by that?"

She sighed in exasperation. "I don't know! That stunt you pulled with the pants… You're just so… Why can't you just be like everyone else?"

That shut me up. I just stared at her, struggling to recognize my best friend. How long had she kept that bottled up?

She picked up her tray and breathed hard through her

nostrils. "I think…I think we should maybe stop spending so much time together."

"You're my best friend," I said, simply.

Maisie shrugged. She just stood there looking down at me, and for the first time ever, I felt that she was really, actually looking *down* on me. She was going to make me say it, wasn't she? "You don't want to be best friends anymore?"

She stared down at her tray and shook her head. The tray was shaking a little bit. The yogurt cup fell on its side and the spoon fell to the floor. Maisie walked away without picking it up.

I leaned over and picked up the spoon, placing it on my own tray. I looked around to see if anyone had been watching our conversation, but people must have stopped paying attention when Jade and Chelsea walked away from the table.

I stared into space, trying to make sense of what had just happened. My best friend had just well and truly unfriended me. All because of some stupid party. But maybe that wasn't the whole truth. Maisie wasn't the kind of person to make rash decisions like that. She liked to think about things from every possible angle before making up her mind. So she had probably been thinking about this for a long time, working up the courage to tell me. Chelsea and Jade had just given her the perfect opportunity.

Maisie and I had been friends for six years. More than half of my life. What would my life look like without Maisie by my side? I couldn't even begin to picture it.

Thinking about what could have happened if I'd told her about The Secret made me feel jumpy and anxious. Thank goodness I'd been sensible enough to keep my mouth shut. It was the only thing comforting me as I sat alone, surrounded by people who didn't care.

I don't need her, anyway. Best friends are more trouble than they're worth.

I've always been good at kidding myself.

=

"I thought Maisie was coming over today?" Mamma said, twisting the cap off a jar of cayenne pepper and sprinkling it into the chili that was bubbling away on the stove.

I checked my watch. It was almost six o'clock. Maisie would be on her way to Chelsea's party. "Mmm?" I pretended that I'd been too busy scruffling Garibaldi's ears to listen to the question.

"I said, isn't Maisie supposed to be coming over?" Mamma stirred the chili (always clockwise—she says it tastes better that way).

Garibaldi lay down on the floor, exposing his tummy for me to rub. He was too far away for me to reach, so I tickled him with my toes. He gave me this look, as if to say, "You call *that* a tummy rub?"

"Liv, I'm talking to you!"

The doorbell rang and Garibaldi went wild, barking and wagging his tail so hard it looked like it might fly off. I ran out of the kitchen, shouting, "I'll get it!" Enzo clattered down the stairs. It was an ongoing contest to see who got to the door first, and we kept score. Enzo had more points than I had, but only because he usually lurked in his bedroom to listen for the gate creaking open. He got there first this time, slamming his hand on the front door. On the other side of the door, a voice said, "Heavens!" When he opened it, Gram was there on the front step, holding her hand up to her chest as if she were worried about her heart.

"Will you two stop this nonsense before you kill me?"

"Sorry, Gram," we said in unison.

When Gram gave me a hug, Enzo did a little victory dance and mouthed the word "loser" at me. Garibaldi wanted a hug from Gram too, but she was having none of it. "Down, boy! Down!" she said. "That's a good boy. No! I said *down*!"

Gram always acts annoyed when Garibaldi jumps up at her like that, but you can tell she loves it, even though he managed to knock her flat on her back one time. She always brings him a dog biscuit, which is a bit unfair because she hardly ever brings Enzo and me anything.

We went to the kitchen and Mamma put water on to boil for tea. Mom wouldn't be home for half an hour, so we were allowed to open a bag of popcorn to hold us over until dinner.

You'd have thought that Gram arriving would have been enough to make Mamma forget all about Maisie, but it wasn't. She asked a third time, and there was no ignoring it now.

"Maisie and I aren't friends anymore." I thought I sounded pretty cool about the whole thing, like I wasn't even bothered. Everyone reacted as if I'd just told them that Maisie had been devoured by a mob of zombie penguins. Even Enzo stopped stuffing popcorn into his face, at least for a second.

Mamma put the lid back on the pot of chili and sat down between Gram and me. "What happened?"

When I didn't answer she took my hand in hers. "*Topolino?*" That's what Mamma calls me when I'm tired, sad, or ill. It means "little mouse" in Italian.

I moved my hand away and grabbed a handful of popcorn. I even managed a casual sort of shrug. "We just grew apart, I suppose."

Mamma exchanged a look with Gram. I hate it when

adults do that. It's like they have some sort of secret conversation going on and we're not allowed to be a part of it. "Okaaay," said Mamma. "Did you fight about something?"

"No." The lie was easy to tell. Just one word.

Gram took a sip of her tea. "I'm sure you two will make up soon. I remember when I was your age. I was always arguing with my friends about this and that! It never lasted."

Enzo grinned and rushed over to get the box we keep under the kitchen bulletin board. He opened it and held it out to Gram. "Pay up!"

"What did I…? Oh, that's not fair!"

Mamma smiled at her. "You know the rules, Frances! You wrote them yourself!"

"All right, all right! Where's my purse?"

The rules were simple. Gram wasn't allowed to say anything that made her sound like an old lady. She was banned from saying things such as, "In my day," and, "They don't make them like they used to," and of course, "When I was your age…" The whole thing was her idea. She's always saying that she feels too young to be a grandmother.

Gram rummaged in her purse for a dollar, while Enzo counted how much was in there. "Fourteen bucks...and this makes fifteen! We're going to be rich, Liv!"

=

No one mentioned Maisie again until bedtime. This time it was Mom—Mamma had clearly given her the lowdown at some point in the evening. She came to tuck me in, even though I've told her again and again that I'm far too old for that sort of thing. She never listens, probably because she knows that I *like* being tucked in. I'm not sure I'd be able to get to sleep without it.

"Do you want to talk about what happened with Maisie? You know you can talk to me about *anything*," she said as she sat down on the edge of the bed.

"There's nothing to talk about," I said, attempting a smile.

"*Liv*..." I recognized that tone of voice. It was the one she uses when she knows I'm lying to her.

I turned over so that I was facing away from her. "I don't *want* to talk about it."

She touched my shoulder gently. "If you've said something to upset Maisie, you can always apologize. You know that, don't you? It's never too late to say you're sorry."

That was the last straw. I lost my temper, big-time. I jumped out of bed and shouted at Mom. "What makes you think *I* said anything to upset *her*? Why does everything have to be *my* fault? I'm sick of it!"

Mom stood too, holding up her hands in surrender. "I'm sorry, sweetheart, I didn't mean anything by it. Now just...just calm down so we can talk about this. There's no need for—"

"No need for *what*? No need for me to lose my temper? WILL PEOPLE STOP SAYING THAT! I HATE IT!" I was yelling now, at the top of my lungs. I wanted to stop, but I couldn't. There's nothing I can do when I get like that, or at least that's how it feels. I'm not in control. It's scary.

Mamma came bursting into the room, so now it was two against one. “Shh! You’ll wake up Enzo! What’s going on in here?” she asked, but Mom and I didn’t answer. We just stood there glaring at each other.

“Okay, it looks like someone is in dire need of a hug.” Mamma held her arms out wide, smiling. It usually works, that little trick. It’s hard to be angry when someone’s hugging you, particularly when that someone is Mamma. She’s just so *warm*, that’s what everyone says about her. But I wasn’t falling for it this time.

I huffed my way over to the bed and pulled the duvet right over my head. “I don’t want a hug. Just… Go away. Both of you.”

There was a pause and I wondered if they were whispering or just shrugging their shoulders. I expected Mom or Mamma to come over and pull back the covers—to chew me out for being so rude—but they didn’t. They just left the room, turning out the light as they went. “Sleep tight, *topolino*,” Mamma whispered into the darkness.

I cried. Finally.

After a few minutes, Garibaldi came scratching at the bedroom door. I dragged myself up off the bed to let him in my room. I helped him up onto the bed, put my arms around him, and cried into his fur. He licked my face in sympathy, or maybe just because he liked the taste of my tears.

It was a long time before I fell asleep. I felt ashamed. Guilty, too.

I was miserable. But why did I have to take that misery out on the only people who actually cared about me? And if I couldn't even manage to tell them about this, how could I ever tell them about *me*?

CHAPTER 15

My first thought after I woke up was, "Maisie was right. Maybe I *should* try to be more like everyone else."

My second thought was, "No. Maybe I should try to be a little more *me*."

(Actually, my very first thought was that I needed to pee, but that doesn't sound dramatic.)

You feel like tiptoeing on the morning after a big argument. You're not quite sure if you're going to launch right back into where you left off in the argument, or whether a few hours of sleep will have miraculously solved everything.

Luckily, it seemed like sleep had done the trick that Sunday. Everyone acted as if nothing was wrong. The moms didn't ask me to apologize, and Enzo was nice to me. Even Garibaldi was better behaved than usual, limiting himself to one single smelly fart over breakfast. (Mind you, it was at least three times more toxic than usual, which made it the same as three individual farts. That was Enzo's theory anyway. He used to draw graphs of Garibaldi's gas. He called it the Fart Chart. I pretended to disapprove, but it was actually quite useful because it helped us remember which foods we should avoid giving Gari under the table.)

At lunchtime, Mamma's phone rang. It was sitting on the table so we could all see that the display read, "Maurizio." Mamma stared at the phone for a few seconds before grabbing it and rushing out of the room. I think Mom was thinking the same thing as me—that it was bad news. I'm pretty sure Enzo wasn't thinking anything much at all, except maybe wondering if he could nab the last potato while no one was looking. Gari was snoozing at my feet, blissfully unaware of anything other than his doggy dreams.

I held my breath when Mamma came back into the room. She put the phone back down on the table and sighed. "He's doing better. He's eating, at least."

"That's wonderful news," said Mom as she stood up to put her arm around Mamma.

I got up and hugged Mamma too.

When the three of us sat back down again, the last potato was gone.

=

I spent the afternoon in my room. I told the moms I was doing homework, but I was working on something much more important than that: phase two of the mission to be allowed to wear pants at Bankridge. I wasn't going to quit just because phase one had ended with Mrs. McCready being mad at me and Jade laughing at me.

I decided that the mission really needed a name. Mostly because I needed something to write at the top of the page in my super-secret planning notebook.

It took me a good twenty minutes to come up with a name I was finally happy with, but I got there in the end:

THE PANTS PROJECT

I spent hours doing research on the laptop. I gathered all the evidence I could, scribbling notes and then writing them out more neatly and marking the important parts with my green highlighter.

Phase two was simple: I was going to talk to the principal. The moms had been meaning to call him, and I knew they would if I asked. But I didn't want to bother them with everything going on with Mamma's father. *Not after the way I behaved last night.*

So I was going to present my arguments to Mr. Lynch on Monday. If that didn't work, it would be time for phase three. Mr. Lynch seemed like a reasonable man, if a little scary-looking. I think it's his pointy nose that does it. It looks like it's been put through a pencil sharpener. He's very tall and has this tendency to peer down his nose at you, like he's lining you up in his sights.

I did some research on Mr. Lynch too. I didn't want to leave anything to chance. I found out that he'd only been at Bankridge for just over a year. He was almost as new as I was! He'd been vice principal at a middle school upstate before he came to Bankridge. I took that as a good sign. Surely, he would be keen to make some changes at Bankridge, now that he was the one in charge. I looked at the website of his old school and a smile spread across my face when I saw that there was no uniform policy. Everyone was free to wear whatever they wanted to wear.

I went to sleep a lot happier that night. I'd barely been able to hide my excitement at dinner. Mom even said, "You're plotting something, aren't you?" I just smiled and mimed zipping my lips closed. That made it quite hard to eat my pasta, so I had to mime unzipping them again. I wanted to wait and tell the moms when I had good news. I hoped they would be proud of me. Maybe it would help make up for how mean I'd been to them on Saturday night. (It didn't occur to me that a better way to make it up to the moms might be saying sorry for losing my temper. Oops.)

CHAPTER 16

Monday didn't start so well. When I walked into homeroom, Maisie was sitting on the back desks with Jade and Chelsea. Maisie didn't look at me, even when Jade loudly said, "*Urgh!* What's that smell? Oh. It's *her*. If *her* is even the right word."

That shook me up a little bit. Not the part about me smelling—that was pathetic. I think that even Enzo stopped using "you smell" as an insult when he was around five. It was the other part that bothered me. Jade couldn't possibly know about The Secret, though. She was probably just talking about my haircut. *Pathetic.*

I was shocked to see Maisie sitting with those girls,

but at the same time I *wasn't* shocked. You know when you're reading a story or watching a movie and you can tell what's going to happen next? (Like when a character is really happy, you know something bad is going to happen. Unless it's right at the end of the book or the movie. People are allowed to be happy—and *stay* happy—then.) As soon as I knew that Maisie was going to Chelsea's party, I had a funny feeling. Why else would she be so keen to drop me as a friend? It was obvious that Jade and Chelsea would never be friends with her while she was still friends with me. She'd decided that it was worth dropping me in order to get in with them.

I sat at my desk while everyone else chattered away. Chelsea's party was the main topic of conversation. She'd arrived in a limousine, apparently.

I've never been in a limo. I have been in a hearse, though. Before Granddad's funeral, I snuck into the shiny black car with the coffin inside. There had been something urgent that I'd wanted to say to Granddad, but as soon as I was sitting next to the glossy wooden box with the gleaming gold handles, the urgent thing flew right out of my head. I think that's when it hit me that he was actually gone. The driver wasn't too happy when he found me crawling around next to the coffin, but he didn't tell the moms. He was a pretty cool guy.

So everyone seemed to be talking about how amazing the party had been. Chelsea and Jade were talking very loudly, probably for my benefit. There was a lot of exaggerated laughter. Maisie's much quieter laugh mixed in with the other two. I told myself it was fine. It was her loss. I didn't need her. And anyway, my secret was safer now that I didn't have a best friend.

I was relieved when Jacob finally arrived. He stopped to talk to some people on the way over to our desk. It was so easy for him—talking to people, I mean. It was natural. Probably because people actually *liked* him.

"Hey." He slumped down into his chair, dropping his bag on the floor with a thump.

"Hey." I noticed he wore a black brace on his right wrist. "Skateboarding injury?"

Something flickered in his eyes before he coughed and

nodded. "Yeah...I was trying a new trick...a kickflip. And I failed epically, obviously."

"Does it hurt?"

"Nah, it's not too bad. Mom made me wear this. You know what moms are like. Anyway, did you have a fun weekend?"

I narrowed my eyes. "Is that supposed to be funny?"

"Um...if it was, it would be a pretty bad joke, don't you think? *Did you have a fun weekend?* Definitely not hilarious. At all."

"You know what I'm talking about," I said, but from the baffled look on his face, it was clear that he didn't. I tried again, looking over my shoulder before whispering, "The party? The one everyone and their dog was invited to except for me and Marion Meltzer?" Marion walked in at that moment, making a beeline straight for her table, not talking to anyone—standard operating procedure for her.

"Oh, *that*? Did you hear about the limo? Who has a pink limo at their twelfth birthday party? Does Chelsea think she's a Kardashian?"

I shrugged. "It must have been a decent party, though. I heard there was a DJ from a nightclub in the city."

Now it was Jacob's turn to shrug. "Must be nice if your parents can afford to fork out thousands of dollars just to have some terrible music that makes your ears bleed."

"I bet the food was good, though."

"Who cares? It's hardly worth it—going to Chelsea's party just to get some decent food. You'd be better off going to Red Lobster."

"So you didn't enjoy it then?"

"Enjoy what?" He tilts his head, looking confused again.

I couldn't help myself. I rapped his forehead with my knuckles. "Hello? Is there anyone at home?" It's something I do to Enzo all the time and he hates it. Jacob didn't seem to like it any more than Enzo and swatted my hand away.

"The party. You didn't enjoy the party." I said the words slowly, like I was explaining something to Enzo.

"What are you talking about? I didn't even *go* to the stupid party!"

Oh.

He told me he'd been invited. Of course he had. Jade had kept pestering him about it, saying the two of them should go together. Even if he'd wanted to go to the party, that would have been enough to put him off for sure. He said he broke the news to Chelsea on Friday afternoon, who responded by saying, "I suppose you've got something better to do."

Jacob told me exactly what he'd said to her, "Yeah, I do, actually. My dog's got a bladder infection and I have to try and get a urine sample from him."

Jade hadn't understood what he was trying to say. "That's not better than Chelsea's party."

Jacob told me he just smiled and said, "That's what you think."

I wish I'd been there.

Now I didn't feel as bad about not going to Chelsea's party. It sort of felt like Jacob and I were in it together somehow. It was a nice feeling.

CHAPTER 17

The principal has an open-door policy. Sometimes. Every Monday during lunch, any student is allowed to see him about anything at all. I figured that had to be a good sign—that he was willing to listen to the students.

"COME IN!"

I had no idea why Mr. Lynch was shouting. His chair was only a couple of feet away from the door, which was wide open. Having an open door is the first (and most important) rule of an open-door policy.

"Mr. Lynch?"

"That's my name, don't wear it out!" He said, and then he laughed way too loudly.

I think I was supposed to laugh too, but I didn't. "There's something I'd like to talk to you about. Something really important."

His eyes widened at that, but I could tell he was just making fun of me. "Well, in that case, you'd better take a seat." He gestured to the comfy-looking floral blue chair next to his desk. The chair was wedged between the desk and a gray filing cabinet, and it looked as out of place as I felt. It sagged under my weight, sort of swallowing me up and making me feel small and useless. Mr. Lynch was sitting on a normal office chair, so he was able to look down his pointy nose at me.

"So. What can I do for you, Miss…?"

I didn't mind that Mr. Lynch didn't know my name. I still found it hard to remember some of the teachers' names, and he had *a lot* more names to remember than I did. But I didn't like the "Miss," obviously. "Spark. Liv…Olivia Spark, sir."

"Spark…" And there was something about the way he

said my name that made me wonder if Mrs. McCready had told him about my attempted pants rebellion after all. Or maybe he remembered my name from when Mr. Eccles sent Jade to his office.

I took my notes out of my bag, feeling my hands shake a little. That wasn't good. I wanted Mr. Lynch to think I was calm and confident—the kind of person he could do business with.

"What do we have here, Olivia? This all looks rather interesting, I must say."

I smiled as my confidence inflated just a little bit—enough to allow me to start talking. "Well, Mr. Lynch. It's about the school's uniform policy. I'm sure you know as well as I do how old-fashioned it is. There was no uniform policy at your last school, was there?"

He looked at me blankly. I was doing it all wrong, so I tried to start again. "Boys wear pants and I think girls should be allowed to wear pants too." *Not that I'm actually a girl, but that's another story.* It was best to keep things simple. For now.

"Well," said Mr. Lynch as he leaned back in his chair

and crossed his legs so that I could see his hairy ankle above his purple socks.

I wasn't quite sure what that meant. I couldn't tell if it was a good "well" or a bad "well." So I decided it would be best if I just forged ahead and said everything I had to say as quickly as possible. I said that skirts weren't practical, that they were cold in winter (even when you wear itchy, woolly tights), and that last week I'd seen some eighth-grade boys trying to look up a girl's skirt when she went up the stairs. I didn't mention that the girl in question was Jade Evans.

When I'd run out of things to say, and checked my notes for anything I might have missed, I sat back in my chair and waited for Mr. Lynch to speak. He was nodding slowly, like one of those plastic dogs you can stick to the dashboard of your car. Nodding had to be a good sign, right?

"Well," he said *again*. "You've clearly done a lot of thinking about this issue, Miss Spark. I'm impressed." He smiled at me, and I smiled back. This was going better than I'd hoped it would.

"Does that mean you'll consider it then? Changing the uniform policy?"

He was still smiling when he said, "No."

"No? I don't understand. You said you were impressed."

"And I was. I *am*. But I'm afraid there are many, many changes that need to be made here at Bankridge. The list is literally as long as my arm." He held up his arm to demonstrate exactly how long that was. "It's a question of priorities, Miss Spark. And my number one priority is providing my students with the best possible education."

"Oh."

"So I'm sure you can appreciate the position I'm in."

"But what about the boys who were looking up that girl's skirt?"

"Can you tell me their names?"

I shook my head.

"Well, then I'll keep a lookout for that in future."

Mr. Lynch stood up and gestured toward the door. "So if that's everything…?" He peered down his nose at me.

"I...so you're not even going to consider it?"

His smile wavered. "I didn't say that. We may well review the uniform policy in a few years' time."

"But you don't even need to *do* anything! Just say that girls can wear pants. All you need to do is mention it in assembly and change it on the website, which I can do for you if you don't know how. I could even get some posters printed to put around the school to remind everyone."

His smile was completely gone now. "Miss Spark, I'm afraid you've heard my final word on the matter. Now, if you wouldn't mind, I have other matters to attend to." He walked over to the door and gestured to it again, just to make sure I knew exactly where it was and how to use it.

I didn't move. My legs wouldn't let me. "But, sir! Please! I can't..." My voice wobbled so I took a deep gulp of air to try to get it under control. "I can't bear to wear this stupid thing for much longer. I hate it!" I may have slightly shouted the last part. I didn't mean to. I never *mean* to shout. It just sort of happens. It's like someone uses the remote control to turn up my volume as soon as I actually care about something. And I really, really cared about this—if only I could do a better job of expressing it.

It was inevitable, really. "I'll thank you not to raise your voice, young lady," said Mr. Lynch. I've always hated being called "young lady." It makes me want to smash things.

I got up from the chair and shoved my notes and papers back into my bag, not bothering to fold them. I swung the bag over my shoulder, narrowly missing a trophy that was on top of the filing cabinet. I briefly considered lobbing the trophy at Mr. Lynch's head, but with my luck he would end up dead and I would have to go to jail, and that would suck. (Although, with Mr. Lynch dead, there would have to be a new principal and maybe *that* one would change the stupid uniform policy, which wouldn't make any difference to me because I would be stuck wearing my prison uniform, whatever *that* might be.)

I was ready to leave the room without saying

anything else. I was determined not to thank Mr. Lynch. Sometimes you thank people by accident, even though you don't really mean it. The word just slips out because you're so used to having to be polite to people. It's the same with "sorry." I say that all the time when people barge into me on the street.

I walked straight past Mr. Lynch without looking up at his silly pointy nose and was out of the room and halfway down the corridor when he called to me. "It can't be that bad, surely?" I turned to see him leaning on the door frame. "Wearing a skirt, I mean."

I knew what he wanted me to say. He wanted me to say that he was right, and I didn't mind wearing a skirt. It was just some silly idea I'd had, and I'd probably forget all about it in a few days.

"Actually, sir, it *is* that bad. How would you like it?"

He shook his head. "Now you're just being silly."

I looked over my shoulder to see if anyone else was around and then took a few steps back toward him. "I'm not trying to be silly. You're saying that *you* wouldn't like to wear a skirt, so why should *I* have to?"

He was getting annoyed now; I was pushing my luck. "Because you're a girl!"

I bet if I told him the truth there and then, he wouldn't have listened. It's all about what people can see, isn't it? And Mr. Lynch didn't see who I was. He saw a girl.

"It's not that simple, sir." I kept my voice calm, purposely keeping the volume down.

He sighed so loudly that it was as if someone had punctured him with a needle, letting all the air escape in one big *whoosh*. "Why do I get the feeling that I haven't heard the last of this?"

I nearly smiled then, but I didn't. I was deadly serious. "Because you haven't, *sir*."

CHAPTER 18

It was Thursday afternoon and Enzo and I were having a competition to see how many olives we could stuff into our mouths. It's not as gross as it sounds. It's not like we put the olives back in the plastic tubs for people to buy. *That* would be gross. We usually sneak out into the alley at the back of the shop to see who can spit the olives the furthest. Enzo's the champion when it comes to spitting. I don't know why I even bother trying to compete. But when it comes to stuffing olives into our mouths, there's no beating me.

The moms and Dante always get onto us when they catch us playing Olive Face, so we have to be careful to only do it when they're not paying attention. Still, they usually know something's up when Mr. Kellerman comes in for his weekly tub of lemon olives and there aren't enough left. It just so happens that lemon olives are the best ones to use for a game of Olive Face. The sourness adds another dimension to the challenge.

Dante was home sick and Mom was at the dentist getting a root canal. Mamma was busy on the phone in the storeroom. It was my job to alert her if a customer came into the deli.

We were in the middle of round three. Enzo's mouth was stuffed full and he was breathing hard through his nose. He looked ridiculous, but I guess I must have looked ridiculous too. I plucked another olive from the tub—the one that would mean I would beat Enzo (*again*). It was a big one too, just to emphasize my victory.

I pushed the olive into my mouth just as the bell above the door tinkled. *A customer!* Enzo and I ducked down beneath the counter, cheeks bulging like hamsters munching on marbles. He pointed at me and then pointed at whoever was now on the other side of the counter. I shook my head, pointing at him. In an unspoken agreement (well, it had to be unspoken), we decided to settle the matter with a speedy game of rock-paper-scissors. I lost.

I stood up and tried to arrange my mouth in something close to a smile, and then I realized that I knew the customer.

Jacob was standing on the other side of the counter, looking about as surprised as I felt. "Hi."

I held up a finger to indicate for him to wait a second. Then I ducked down again and spat the lemon olives into the bin. Enzo did a little victory dance, which was some feat given that he was still crouching down. Then he spat his olives into the same bucket.

I stood up again, my cheeks feeling oddly stretched and tingly. "Hi. What are you doing here?"

Jacob's face was red, and he was blatantly hiding something behind his back.

"My mom asked me to get some cheese. She's in a café down the street. I forgot you said your mom and…mom run a deli."

It was painfully obvious that Jacob had been about to say "dad," but he'd caught himself at the last second.

"What's that behind your back?"

"Nothing."

"Show me!"

It was a walking stick.

"I never took you for the English-gentleman type! What's next? A bowler hat? You look so fancy!"

He didn't laugh. "It's my mom's." He pulled on the end of the stick and started folding it up. By the time, he was finished, it was barely longer than a pencil.

"That's pretty cool. Why does she need a walking stick?"

"She has this…condition. She doesn't have to use it very—"

"Hi! I'm Enzo!" Enzo sprang up from his hiding place, making Jacob jump. That kid always did have impeccable timing.

Jacob laughed to cover his embarrassment. "It's nice to meet you, Enzo."

"Who are you? Are you Liv's *boyfriend*?" Enzo stretched out the word, enjoying himself.

I kicked him in the shin. Not very hard, but hard enough to (hopefully) stop him from being so annoying. Jacob just laughed and said, "No, we're just friends."

That was weird. *Good* weird though. I suppose we *were* friends. I'd found a real-live actual friend at Bankridge Middle School without even noticing.

We let Jacob come behind the counter to get a better look at the cheese choices. Enzo recommended the gruyère, and I recommended the taleggio. Jacob hemmed and hawed before deciding he'd take some of both (even though his mom had asked him to get Monterey Jack). Enzo ran to get Mamma to slice the cheese. We weren't allowed to use the cheese slicer, even though I'd promised to stop joking about slicing off Enzo's fingers.

Mamma was happy to meet Jacob, and she didn't even try to hide it. She let him try the cheeses before he bought them, and she said he should come over to our house for dinner one day soon. Jacob thanked her and said he would like that. He was clearly much better at talking to adults than I was because he knew all of the right things to say, and it didn't even come across as fake.

I could tell that Enzo liked Jacob. He kept asking him questions about basketball, skateboarding, and gaming. Jacob didn't seem to mind at all.

"Your family's really nice," Jacob said as I walked him to the door. Mamma and Enzo were having a "discussion" about whether Enzo would be allowed to go to the skate park this weekend. Jacob had wisely taken the opportunity to make his getaway.

"Weird, you mean."

Jacob shrugged. "Everybody's weird. My mom's obsessed with One Direction."

"OK, that is definitely weird." I followed Jacob outside. "Anyway, I guess I'll see you tomorrow."

"I guess you will. And tell your mom I'll keep an eye out for Enzo at the skate park if he wants to come down on Sunday."

"I call her 'Mamma' because she's Italian."

Jacob nodded. "And what do you call your other mom?"

"You'll *never* guess," I said with a smile. Then I decided to put him out of his misery and tell him that she's just Mom.

"Will she give me free samples of cheese too?" Jacob grinned.

"Probably. I bet she'll take pity on you when I tell her your mom is in love with Harry Styles."

He guffawed at that. "How do you know she likes Harry?"

I laughed. "Just a hunch."

When Jacob walked away, I noticed that the sidewalk was wet and that he was walking very, very slowly. Halfway down the street, he looked back over his shoulder. He gave a quick wave then set off again, a little faster this time.

=

Mamma told Mom all about Jacob at dinner. We were having chicken cacciatore—one of my favorites. Poor Mom was only having a glass of water because her mouth was still numb from the dentist; we laughed every time she tried to talk.

Between the two of them (with added input from Enzo), they decided that I should invite Jacob over for dinner on Saturday.

"But that's only two days away!"

"So what?" The moms said in unison.

I was just about coming to terms with the idea when Mom had to go and ruin it. "It will be nice for you to have a friend over." At least that's what I *think* she said. It sounded more like, "Ih wih bih ice fuh ou ou ah a hwend oha."

"What's that supposed to mean?"

Mom shrugged and Mamma took over. "I don't think it's supposed to mean anything, Liv. It's just that you haven't had anyone over in a while. It's good that you've made friends with Jacob. He seems like a really nice boy."

"He's OK, I suppose."

The moms shared a smile when I said that. Mamma helped herself to some more salad and suggested I invite Maisie to come too.

"No!" I said, a little more forceful than I'd intended. I figured it was time to tell them that Maisie wouldn't be coming over again—ever. That Maisie and I hadn't made up, and never would. I didn't tell the whole story, obviously. I just said that she'd found some new friends who weren't very nice. Mamma asked if they weren't very nice to *me*, or just in general. I admitted that sometimes they were a little mean to me. When you're trying to cover something up (like the fact that you're being bullied because you have two moms), it's better to tell *some* of the truth (that some girls are being slightly mean to you, but you don't know why).

Mom wanted to call the school to get the girls to stop, and Mamma agreed with her. Enzo was too busy licking his plate to care, and Garibaldi was too busy politely waiting for someone to throw him some chicken. Gari *would* have cared though—if only he could have understood. I'm sure of it.

I wiped my mouth with my napkin and took a sip of water. In my calmest, most grown-up voice, I said that I would prefer to handle the situation on my own. I said that it was nothing to worry about because they were just a bunch of silly, immature little kids, and I really didn't care whether they liked me or not.

It took a while for me to convince the moms, and they made me promise to come and talk to them if things got any worse, or if I changed my mind. Mamma said that I should think very hard about whether I wanted them to do anything about it. She said that *I* might be strong enough to deal with the mean girls, but what if they picked on someone who wasn't? Marion popped into my mind when she said that. She *never* talked back when Jade said mean things to her. I told Mamma I'd think about it.

When we were clearing the table, Mamma said that it was a shame about Maisie. "She always seemed like such a nice girl." Mom muttered something that I couldn't hear because the kettle was starting to boil. From the look on Mamma's face, I don't think it was anything good.

If my suspicions were right (and I think they were), it was sort of reassuring that Mom had said something mean about Maisie. It reminded me that Maisie was the one with the problem, not me. She was the one who'd changed all of a sudden. I'd stayed exactly the same—as far as *she* knew, anyway.

CHAPTER 19

Jacob seemed excited about coming over for dinner. He asked if we always ate pizza and pasta in our house, and I told him that Italian cooking wasn't all about pizza and pasta. Then I had to admit that we were in fact having pizza for dinner on Saturday, which made him laugh.

He stopped laughing when Jade and Chelsea walked into the classroom, closely followed by another girl. I almost didn't recognize Maisie. She was blond, for one thing, and wearing *a lot* of makeup.

She looked bizarre, but she clearly didn't think so. She sauntered into the room with her back straight and her head held high. When she noticed me staring, her shoulders slumped a little and she hurried the rest of the way to her table.

You're not allowed to wear "excessive makeup" at Bankridge, but none of the teachers ever enforce *that* rule. No one seems to care. In fact, girls who don't wear makeup are definitely in the minority. If I'm being honest, Maisie's hair didn't look that bad. It sort of suited her. Maybe. A little bit. The makeup was stupid, though. Her eyelashes were all clumped together, like spiders trapped in an oil slick. She should have asked Jade for some lessons instead of just trying to copy her and hoping for the best.

Jacob raised his eyebrows at me and whispered, "Looks like Jade's tried to clone herself. She must have gotten someone else to do the tricky DNA stuff."

He started drawing right away. He drew a conveyor belt coming out of a huge machine with lots of buttons and levers on it. Three boxes housing identical dolls sat on top of the conveyor belt. Each box had a name written on it: Jade, Chelsea, and Maisie. Maisie's box was the last one on the belt, just emerging from the machine. I watched as Jacob wrote "new and improved?" on the box with the Maisie doll inside.

=

Friday was a big day. It was time for phase three of the Pants Project—the petition.

I'd had the petition brainwave when Mom mentioned some online petition she'd signed against cruelty to animals. She said the government would *have* to do something, now that there were so many signatures. I thought that a petition seemed like the perfect way to drum up some support for my cause and force Mr. Lynch to take action.

For the past few days, I'd been sitting with Jacob and his friends at lunch. It had started with Jacob bringing his tray over to where I sat, alone in the corner. Then a couple of his friends sat with us a few minutes later. Things seemed to be so much simpler with boys. They accepted me because Jacob accepted me. They knew all about the moms (I don't think there was anyone in the entire school who *didn't* know by then), but they didn't seem to care. On Thursday, Miguel had whispered to me that his older brother is gay. I didn't quite know what to say to that, so I just said, "Cool," in what I hoped was a friendly way.

While Alex, Sav, and Miguel were busy talking about something (apparently) hilarious that had happened in their PE class (something to do with a wedgie, I think?), I showed Jacob the petition. I'd already told him about the Pants Project and how annoying Mr. Lynch had been. He was impressed that I hadn't backed down in Lynch's office.

He looked carefully at the petition and nodded his approval. "Nice job on the lettering."

I was proud of it. I'd copied it from my favorite comic book. It looked big, bold, and *important*. I asked Jacob if he thought it would be better if I did the whole thing on the computer and printed it out.

"Nah, it's better this way. More personal. People are more likely to sign it if they can see that it really matters to you." While I was thinking that over, he signed his name. "There. One down, a few hundred to go."

"Do you think I should sign it too?"

"Um, *yeah*!" he laughed. So I signed my name underneath his.

Jacob managed to get the boys to shut up, and I told them about the petition. Sav said that he *liked* that the girls wore skirts, but a steely glare from me shut him up. They all signed it, bringing the count up to five signatures. Five signatures in less than five minutes seemed pretty good to me. Annoyingly, the bell rang signaling the end of lunch before I had a chance to try for more signatures.

I'd decided that I probably needed to get at least half of the students to sign the petition in order to get Mr. Lynch to take it seriously. Five hundred total students meant that I needed more than 250 signatures on my petition. It wasn't going to be easy, that was for sure.

=

We had Mrs. McCready last period on Friday. She reminded us that Back-to-School Night was coming up and asked for volunteers to help out.

Jacob's hand shot up. "We'll do it, Mrs. M!" Now you'd have to know Jacob to know just how *un*-Jacob-like this was, so you're going to have to trust me when I say that. Even Mrs. McCready was shocked. "Er, okay, lovely! Thank you, Jacob. And thank *you*, Olivia. I take it you're willing to lend a hand too?"

I nodded—anything to get the attention away from me.

"I'll help too, Mrs. McCready," said a syrupy voice from the back of the room.

"And me!"

Excellent. Jade and Chelsea. The only thing worse than that would be…

"I'm sure Maisie would like to volunteer too!" said Jade. I turned around to see Maisie nodding, trying to look enthusiastic.

"Why did you do that?" I hissed at Jacob.

"Isn't it obvious?"

"No!"

"We need her."

"Who?"

"McCready!"

I had no idea what he was talking about, so he whispered an explanation. For the Pants Project to succeed, we would need allies (*powerful* allies, according to Jacob). If we got some teachers on our side, it would put extra pressure on Mr. Lynch, and what better way to get Mrs. McCready on our side than being helpful on Back-to-School Night?

It was a decent plan, I had to admit. It hadn't crossed my mind to try to get teachers on our side. I'd just assumed they'd be on Mr. Lynch's side. But Mrs. McCready never wore skirts, so surely she would sympathize, even if she hadn't exactly been thrilled with my attempted pants-skirt combo.

It was starting to feel like Jacob and I were a team, like the whole pants mission wasn't just my crusade anymore. It was really cool, considering there was nothing in it for him. I ignored the tiny voice in the back of my head whispering that it would be better just to tackle it on my own. *The only person you can trust is yourself.* I didn't really believe that. There were three people I trusted 100 percent: Mom, Mamma, and Enzo. Gram too (sometimes). So that made four (maybe three and a half?). And I trusted Garibaldi, which goes without saying. But family and dogs don't really count, do they? You kind of take it for granted that you can trust your family and your dog. Finding other people to trust is tricky. I'd trusted Maisie and look at how *that* had turned out.

CHAPTER 20

Jacob's mom dropped him off at our house late on Saturday afternoon. She waved from the car. She certainly looked normal enough. There was nothing about her to suggest she was a crazed One Direction superfan. She had curly hair, cool glasses, and a friendly smile.

"So this is the famous Garibaldi! Man, you're like three times the size of my dog. Oh, yes you are." I liked that Jacob talked to my dog. I hate it when people ignore him.

Jacob kneeled down to let Gari give him a good sniff. Gari's tail thumped a rapid drumbeat on the floor, and when Jacob held out his hand with the palm facing up, Gari brought up his paw for a high five. Jacob had somehow managed to pick the only trick that my dog knows how to do.

Enzo was practically bouncing off the walls with excitement about Jacob being here. He dragged him up to his room to show off the Lego spaceship he'd built that morning. I kept quiet about the fact that I'd actually built most of the spaceship after Enzo had a total meltdown when he got stuck and didn't understand the instructions. I am *awesome* at building with Legos. My Lego collection is probably my most prized possession. Enzo asks at least once a week if he can have it when I die. Each and every time, I tell him that my Legos will be buried with me. Enzo thinks that a coffin made of Legos would be the best thing ever.

Mom arrived home from Monty's and got to work on the tomato sauce for the pizzas. I could tell straightaway that she liked Jacob. He kept asking if there was anything he could do to help. Parents *love* that.

Mamma had made the pizza dough earlier and left it

to proof. Jacob and I got started on the toppings. I sliced the salami while he sliced the onions. His eyes started watering and I teased him about crying. He played along and pretended that he was overcome with emotion because he was so happy to be here.

It was really nice, actually. The five of us all together in the kitchen. It didn't feel weird adding Jacob into the mix. He seemed to know the right thing to do or say at the right time, and he was excited about pizza. Apparently, his dad had tried to make pizza once, but the base had turned out more like a cookie. I let him tear up the balls of mozzarella even though it's usually my job. Jacob had never even seen real mozzarella before. Of course, that started Mamma off on a *looong* rant about food in this country, which ended with, "And pizza with slices of canned pineapple! What is wrong with you people?"

Jacob was brave enough to say that he actually liked ham and pineapple pizza. Mamma frowned and shook her head. "And here I was starting to like you. Such a shame!" She smiled to let him know that she was only joking—sort of. Mamma said that once he'd tasted *our* pizza, he would never go back to his "heathen ham and pineapple ways."

One bite was all it took. Jacob's eyes widened and he started nodding. That bite was quickly followed by two more. "OK, this is definitely the best pizza I have ever had in my entire life."

Mamma patted his shoulder and smiled smugly. "Of course it is."

Jacob ate *loads.* He sat back in his chair and patted his stomach. "I don't think I could eat another thing."

Mom said, "Not even ice cream?"

"Well, there's always room for ice cream. Different stomach, isn't it? Dessert stomach. Can I come for dinner every day, please?" Jacob smiled winningly.

The moms laughed. "I'm sure your mom would have something to say about that!"

"Nah, she'd be grateful. She hates cooking. Dad's not bad, but he's usually too tired by the time he gets home."

"So why don't *you* cook then?" I asked.

"I'm a little clumsy with a knife. My hands..." Jacob's words drifted off into nothing.

"What about your hands?" I asked.

He shook his head. "Nothing. I tell you what. I'll make dinner for my folks once a week, but only if you promise to give me the recipe for that pizza. The sauce was *epic*."

It might seem like Jacob was sucking up to them, but he wasn't, or at least I didn't think so. He seemed genuinely happy to spend time with us. It made me wonder what it would be like if Jade and Chelsea came over for dinner. How could they think there was anything wrong or weird about my family? We were so normal it was boring. Of course, there was no way on earth I would ever invite those two over to my house. I would rather stick chili peppers up my nose and sniff.

I was scraping the last of my ice cream out of the bowl when Jacob said he thought it was awesome that I'd started the petition. I'd forgotten to tell him not to say anything.

I was worried the moms would think that I was causing

trouble. More than anything in the world, I didn't want them to say that it wasn't important. I was scared that they wouldn't understand just how much it meant to me. I didn't think I'd be able to cope if the moms didn't get it. Plus, I didn't want them to ask any awkward questions about exactly *why* it meant so much to me.

Jacob explained all about it and how Mr. Lynch had said no to changing the uniform policy. "But we're not going to let him win, are we, Liv?"

The moms listened as Jacob told them all about the petition and how many signatures we were hoping to get. He didn't say anything about us helping with Back-to-School Night in order to butter up Mrs. McCready.

When he was finished, Mom reached across the table and put her hand on mine. "I'm so proud of you."

"Why?" I asked quietly.

"You're standing up for what you believe in, and that's important." I should have known Mom would say something like that.

Mamma said, "I can call Mr. Lynch on Monday, Liv. I've been meaning to. It's just with everything going on with my father…I… It's no excuse, though. I'm sorry."

"It's OK. I think this is something I need to do on my own, you know?" As soon as I said the words, I realized they were true. This was *my* fight. Well, mine and Jacob's now.

Mamma smiled. "Your mom's right. I'm proud of you too. You've really grown up over the past few months, haven't you?"

That made me squirm with embarrassment. It's not exactly the kind of thing you want to hear in front of someone from school. Anyway, I was secretly happy because I thought that maybe Mamma was right. I did feel like a different person from the one who'd punched Danny Barber in the face. Don't get me wrong, I didn't regret doing it (not even a little bit), but I think if the same situation came up now I'd handle it differently. Not that the same situation would ever come up again because Maisie had other friends to stick up for her now. Jade would never punch someone, though, would she? She'd just make their lives miserable until they felt like punching *themselves* in the face.

"Awww, Liv's blushing!" You can always count on Enzo to say something really annoying or embarrassing.

Mom took some of the heat off me by asking Jacob why he was helping with the petition. I took the empty ice cream bowls over to the sink, but I listened hard. I was curious too.

"It's important to Liv," he said. "And I guess I wouldn't like it if *I* had to wear a skirt to school, so why should Liv be any different?"

His answer could not have been more perfect. It made me wonder if maybe I could tell him the truth about me. Maybe he would understand, or at least try. The thought of actually saying the words aloud was terrifying, but part of me wanted *someone* to know. I wanted at least one person to see me for who I actually was, instead of who they thought I was. I wanted someone to see the real me.

That night I went to bed feeling that things were definitely (finally) looking up. With Jacob's help, there was a chance that the petition would actually be a success. People liked Jacob. If they knew he was involved with the Pants Project, they were much more likely to support it. And surely there must be girls at school who hated wearing skirts just as much as I did.

CHAPTER 21

After two days of going around with the petition during recess and at lunch, I had just thirty-four signatures. Nine of those were from a table of eighth-grade girls, who were actually nice to me. One of them even said, “Good luck, kid,” which was kind of patronizing, but it was much better than the straight-up mean things that some people had said.

I could just about deal with the eye rolling and smirking. It was harder to cope with people laughing in my face and asking why I wanted to be a boy. Several people said that I *looked* like a boy, which must explain why I wanted to wear pants so badly. If only they knew how right they were.

Marion came up to me after homeroom on Wednesday and asked to sign the petition. While she was signing her name excruciatingly slowly, she whispered, "I hate wearing skirts too."

I nodded distractedly, suddenly aware that Jade, Chelsea, and Maisie were lurking nearby, watching. "Losers: assemble!" Jade crowed, and the other two laughed on cue.

Marion rolled her eyes and muttered, "Ignore her." The very definition of easier said than done. "Is there anything…? I mean, I'd like to help with the petition, if I can. I was wondering if maybe—?"

"Yeah, thanks, but I'm all good. Um, I have to go." I grabbed the petition back and hurried past Jade and the others, leaving Marion to face their taunts alone.

It was nice of her to offer to help, I guess, but Marion was almost as unpopular as I was. If anything, she'd make people *not* want to sign my petition.

Jacob had already offered to come around with me, but I'd stupidly said no. I guess I thought that I should be the one to make this thing happen. By Friday, I was ready to admit defeat. I needed help, after all, and Jacob was definitely a better option than Marion.

The two of us set off on a signature hunt, with me steering Jacob away from Marion's table. I should have been a lot nicer to her when she offered to help, but Jade had really got to me. *Again.* I saw Marion watching us from the other side of the cafeteria. I felt bad, but I had to focus on the job of getting signatures.

After just ten minutes, we had another twenty-two signatures. I was a little annoyed. I didn't mean to be, but it didn't seem fair that people listened to Jacob, but not to me. The stupid uniform rule didn't even affect him! But that's the power of popularity, or maybe that's the power of being seen as a boy. People *listen*. Even though he was only in the sixth grade, the older kids seemed to respect him in a way that they clearly didn't respect me. They thought I was weird, and they didn't take me seriously. I had Jade Evans to thank for that.

Jacob asked what was wrong. He thought I should be happy about the extra signatures. I *was*, but I couldn't explain to him why I was upset. I hadn't told him about the things people had said to me. I hadn't told him about a couple of days ago when a seventh-grader had taken the petition and got his pen ready to sign. Then he stopped and said, "Before I sign, can I ask you a question?" I should have known from the sly smile that slithered across his face that it was going to be bad. "Are you a boy or a girl?" He paused and looked around at his friends, making sure they were all paying attention. "Or something in between?"

I just walked away with my jaw clenched and laughter echoing in my ears.

But Jacob didn't know anything about that. I apologized and thanked him for helping me. "Is it…are you worried about your grandfather? I'm sorry he's so sick."

I didn't know what to say for a second. Enzo must have said something on Saturday—keeping secrets was not his specialty. This wasn't a secret, but still, family stuff is usually private.

"No, it's not that, but thanks. And thanks for helping me today. It was…it was really nice of you."

Jacob shrugged off the compliment. "Anytime."

So by Friday afternoon there were fifty-six signatures—out of the 250 or so we needed for Mr. Lynch to take us seriously. That wasn't bad. Only 194 signatures to go. My eyes roamed down the list of names as Jacob told me about some new trick he was learning on his skateboard.

SpongeBob SquarePants
Chip Munk
Kanye West
ROCKY ROAD

Right. Make that 198 signatures to go.

CHAPTER 22

Mrs. McCready had asked the students helping with Back-to-School Night to stay after school for a few minutes. Everyone else stampeded out of the classroom, leaving me with Jacob and *those* three.

Back-to-School Night was next Thursday, and Mrs. McCready made it very clear that she wanted things to run as smoothly as possible. She picked Jacob and me to be the students who would greet parents at the main entrance to hand out maps so they could find their way around the school. Chelsea and Maisie were in charge of refreshments. So it wasn't going to be so bad. At least I didn't have to be with…

"Actually, on second thought, we should have Jade and Olivia at the main entrance, and Jacob can roam the corridors looking for lost souls."

"But Mrs. McCready..." I started, but stopped when Jacob gave me a sharp look and a tiny but unmistakable shake of the head.

"Yes, Olivia?"

"Um, would it be OK if...I mean, if you don't mind...I'd really prefer it if you called me Liv." Jade snorted in derision. She knew that I'd been about to complain about being paired with her.

"Of course, Olivia! Or *Liv*, rather. You should have asked sooner!"

I felt like an idiot, but at least I was an idiot with a name I didn't despise *quite* so much.

"So is everyone happy about that? Good. Thank you all so much for volunteering. I have a feeling you're going to make Bankridge very proud, and I'm so looking forward to meeting your parents."

I could feel Jade looking at me when Mrs. McCready said that. After a second or two, Jade said, "I'm *so* looking forward to welcoming all of the moms and *dads* to Bankridge," Jade said in that revolting voice she uses whenever she talks to teachers.

Mrs. McCready obviously had no idea what Jade was really getting at. "That's very nice to hear, Jade. All right, we will reconvene on Tuesday just to make sure everyone knows exactly what they should be doing. Have a lovely weekend. And Chelsea? Please remember to actually *do* your math homework this time!"

Mrs. McCready packed up her bag and left the room.

"Are you coming, Liv?" asked Jacob.

We were going to Monty's. The moms had said we could have an early dinner of Epic Sandwiches. That's what we call it when we pile the toppings so high that the filling is at least three times as thick as the bread.

"Are you two going on a *date*?" Jade said in a malicious voice. "Just kidding. *Of course* you're not. I suppose I can see why you like spending so much time with *it*, Jake. Must be just like hanging out with one of the guys." She was pleased with herself, especially when Maisie and Chelsea chimed in with their inane giggles.

Maisie's laughter seemed to be genuine, though. She wasn't laughing just because she was scared of Jade, and that made it hurt even more.

I was ready to ignore Jade, but Jacob turned on her. "You shut your mouth, Jade Evans or I'll..." I'd never seen his face like that before, all dark and stormy.

"You'll *what*? You wouldn't hit a *girl*, would you Jake?" She smiled and blinked, acting all innocent.

"I'm warning you."

"Jacob, it's fine. Just leave it. She's not worth it." It had been hard for me to say those words. Really hard. Especially since I was picturing smashing Jade's face into the whiteboard.

"Yeah, *Jacob*. Why don't you and your little mutant run along now and do whatever it is mutants do? How's the petition going, by the way? And why haven't you asked *us* to sign it? I happen to think that freaks should be able to wear whatever they want. It makes it easier for the rest of us to avoid them." She must have been saving up these insults for a while now because there was no way she was coming up with this stuff on the spot. (And clearly she'd never even read an X-Men comic or seen any of the movies—mutants are *awesome*.)

I grabbed Jacob's arm and pulled him toward the door. If I didn't get out of there right that second, I was worried I might do something I would regret—something Jade would regret even more.

We were halfway out the door when Jade called out, "Bye, *Olivia*! Make sure you tell your mom that I'm really looking forward to meeting her. Your *other* mom too. My dad's been telling me all about *their* kind."

I turned around then. I had to. But I didn't look at Jade's smug face. I ignored her completely. I looked at Maisie. She wouldn't look me in the eyes. She was ashamed. *Good*. After everything my parents had done for her, the fact that she could just stand there and let Jade say those things was too much for me to handle.

I ran from the room.

CHAPTER 23

Jacob didn't manage to catch up with me until I'd reached the school gate. I stomped down the street while he struggled to keep up.

"Liv, I'm so sorry."

"Don't. Stop talking right now."

"What do you mean?"

"I don't want your pity, Jacob Arbuckle, and I don't want to talk about it. So either you pretend that nothing happened, or you can just go straight home."

He stopped walking, so I had to stop too. I felt guilty. "I'm sorry, I just…it's the weekend, and the last thing I want to talk about or even think about is Jade Evans. So please, can we just forget about it?"

Jacob shook his head. "How can you do that? After those things she said?"

I shrugged, staring at the cracked paving stones at my feet. "You get used to it."

"*How?*"

"You just do. After a while you stop listening and stop caring."

I looked and saw that he wasn't buying it. *Fair enough.* I couldn't blame him for not believing me because it wasn't exactly true. The truth is that you *do* care. Of course you do. And it hurts to hear people say those things about you. But the hurt changes, over time. At first, it's sharp and hot, like a fiery dagger stabbing you in the heart, but when you've heard the same insults over and over and over, the pain changes. It becomes a dull, throbbing ache—like a toothache. A sort of background pain that you can ignore for a few minutes at a time, except when you're lying in bed at night, trying to sleep. That's when it really gets to you.

"I don't know why people have to be so mean," Jacob said, shaking his head. He seemed younger somehow, more innocent. He reminded me of Enzo. One of the things I like about Jacob is that he can't even imagine why people are bullies. That must be what it's like to be a nice person. I'm not a nice person, though. Well, I suppose I'm OK most of the time, but definitely not *all* of the time. I had no trouble coming up with reasons why Jade was targeting me: she had to put other people down in order to feel good about herself. I was different and she was bored.

I changed the subject and told Jacob that I might like to try skateboarding someday. I neglected to mention that I'd already tried it once. I borrowed my cousin's skateboard a couple of years ago, but it did not go well. Knees were scraped and bruises blossomed. Still, the topic distracted Jacob, and by the time we reached the deli, he was acting normally again. He'd even managed to convince me to actually give skateboarding another go.

Dante was blasting music from the little stereo behind the counter. He's only allowed to do that when there are no customers. A couple of his friends were sitting at the table next to the door, but they don't really count as real customers because they never buy anything. They just come to the deli to hang out when they're bored or when it's raining.

Dante was behind the counter, slicing big chunks of cheese, wrapping them up in paper, and then weighing them and putting a price label on the package. He looked up and grinned when he saw me. "The Livmeister General!" He always calls me that. I have no idea why. "And this must be Jacob! How's it going, man?"

Jacob smiled and said it was going well. I asked Dante where Mom was, and he said she was at the swimming pool with Enzo and Mamma. I'd forgotten they were going swimming. I felt a pang of sadness. I used to love going to the pool, especially since they put in waterslides. The moms were surprised when I told them I didn't want to go anymore. I said swimming was boring. I said I had better things to do. I'm not sure if they believed me, but they didn't force me to go with them. I already knew how to swim (and was pretty good at it), so they didn't have to worry about me if our car plunged into a fast-flowing river or if I fell off the back of a ferry.

I missed swimming. A lot. I missed diving into the water and gliding along the bottom of the pool, seeing how long I could go without taking a breath. I could swim a whole length without coming up for air, even though it made me feel dizzy and strange.

The truth is, I wouldn't have given up swimming if I'd been able to swim in a pool without other people in it and change my clothes in a room on my own.

The real reason I stopped swimming was simple.

My body was changing. And it felt very, very wrong.

=

Jacob and I settled down to eat our Epic Sandwiches and Dante sat down with his friends. I love the deli most when there are no actual customers. The moms prefer it when it's heaving and the line is out the door. That usually only happens on Saturday mornings when people come in to get their bread and pastries. I suppose it's good that we have busy days, otherwise we wouldn't be able to afford food (and video games). But it's so much better when it's just us in there. Dante's friends count as "us" because I've known them for years. They still refuse to call me by my name, though. To them, I am, and always will be, "Spark Plug." It's not the best nickname in the world, but I seem to be stuck with it.

Jacob managed to eat half of his sandwich before he started to feel sick. "Amateur," I said, going in for another ginormous bite. It's a point of pride that I always—*always*—finish my Epic Sandwich.

I couldn't stop thinking about what Jade had said about meeting the moms. What had her dad said to her? Was he as mean as she was? Maybe that was where Jade got her mean streak. And if that were true, then was it really her fault?

"Do you know what transgender means?" The words were out of my mouth before I even realized it. I quickly looked around to see if Dante and the guys had heard, but the music was way too loud. I turned back to Jacob and tried to smile, as if it was a perfectly normal question to ask.

"Is it when a man dresses up as a woman? Like that guy on TV?"

I didn't say anything. I looked down at the crumbs on my plate. This had been a terrible idea. Why hadn't I kept my mouth shut?

"Why? Liv, are you OK? What's this about?"

I kept staring at my plate. "That's not what it means. It's sort of when a person feels like the way they are on the inside doesn't quite match up with the way they look on the outside. At least, that's how it is for some people, but it's different for everyone… Anyway, what I'm trying to say is that you might look at someone and think you see a boy, but inside, they know that they're actually a girl. Or…"

Jacob leaned closer. "Or what?" he asked, softly.

This was it. I was really going to do it. The moment had snuck up on me when I wasn't paying attention, but I was ready. Kind of. "Or you might look at someone and see a girl, but that's not who they really are."

Jacob didn't say anything. The silence went on for far too long. Eventually, I had to look up. He was watching me.

It was clear from the look on his face that he knew what I was saying. He was just waiting for me to say the words. So I said them. "I think…I *know*…I'm transgender."

It was hard to look at him, but I needed to see his face—his true reaction. You can never hide your true reaction to something, not in that first second or two.

Jacob's face didn't change, not even a little bit. He nodded and said, "OK."

He didn't laugh or look grossed out or seem confused or embarrassed. He just looked…well, he just looked like Jacob.

I laughed shakily. "*OK?* That's all you have to say?"

He shrugged. "What else would you like me to say?"

"I don't know! You're not…freaked out by it?"

"Should I be?" He smiled.

"No!"

"Well, OK then." I kept staring at him until he spoke again. "You're my friend, Liv. That's all that matters to me."

"OK," I whispered.

"I don't want you to think that I don't care about

what you said. I *do* care. But it doesn't change anything. We're still friends, right? Fighting the forces of evil and dress codes of doom?" He smiled that cheeky smile that always gets him out of trouble.

"Right." I smiled back, even though there were tears in my eyes. Good tears.

So that was that. Jacob knew the truth and it was fine. It was the relief that made me cry, I think. He looked a bit embarrassed then. I couldn't blame him. I never knew what to do when people cried in front of me either. Thankfully, I managed to get the tears under control quite quickly, before my face turned red and snot started streaming from my nose.

I cleared my throat. "So, now that that's out of the way… Can I finish your sandwich?"

CHAPTER 24

I walked home from Monty's feeling as if a huge weight had been lifted from my shoulders. I still couldn't believe how well it had gone, and how nice Jacob had been. He even said we should amp up our efforts on the Pants Project.

When we'd said good-bye, he asked if anyone else knew about me being transgender. He didn't say anything when I said no, but he did say that if I ever needed anyone to talk to about it, I could talk to him. "I can't promise to understand it all, or to say the right thing all the time, but I can promise to listen."

The relief was unbelievable. I'd finally told someone. Someone who wasn't Garibaldi. (I'd told Gari ages ago, whispering into his ear. His reaction was almost as good as Jacob's—a big yawn.)

I was practically skipping down the street (which is not something I would ever, ever do, by the way) until I remembered that everything wasn't OK after all. Jade's words were echoing in my head. Back-to-School Night was less than a week away.

I felt sick at the thought of the moms turning up at Bankridge and being greeted by mean looks and snide comments from Jade. And what if her dad said something too? I couldn't think of anything worse. The thought of these people being horrible to my parents...

I couldn't allow it to happen. I wouldn't put them in that position.

I had to make sure they didn't go to Back-to-School Night.

=

They'd already been invited. It was on the kitchen calendar, written in purple in Mom's scrawly handwriting. I just had to figure out a way to *un*invite them.

That was definitely the main reason for not wanting them at Back-to-School Night. I was doing it to protect them. They thought everything was fine and dandy at Bankridge because I'd told them that the mean comments had stopped ages ago. They would be really upset to find out that wasn't true.

OK, so if I'm being completely honest, there was another reason too. It wasn't that I was ashamed of my parents, or that I was embarrassed to be seen with them. I was tired of being a target. It's not exactly fun dealing with the kind of stuff I'd had to deal with, especially when it's happening every single day. The locker room was the worst. I was usually able to change clothes before anyone else came into the locker room, but sometimes a teacher would keep me after class, and I would find myself in the middle of my worst nightmare.

Last week, Chelsea loudly told Jade that she'd seen a bulge in my underwear (I *wish*!). It didn't matter that she was lying because people will believe what they want to believe, and Jade very much wanted to believe that. As she walked past me on the way to the gym, she said to Chelsea and Maisie, "I wouldn't mind so much if they let an *actual* boy in here, but freaks should really have their own separate place to change."

The one consolation was that Maisie didn't laugh. She winced and shook her head, not that Jade noticed since she was already walking away.

The funny thing was that I agreed with Jade. I would love to have my own place to change. Maybe the school would let me, one day, if the moms told them the truth about me. Of course, I'd need to tell the moms first for there to be any chance of that ever happening.

I knew I should stick up for myself more at school. Jade's bullying was getting out of control, and I knew the Pants Project wasn't helping. It was just something else for her to make fun of, but it was important to me and I didn't want anything to jeopardize it. I promised myself that once the project was over and done, I would do something about Jade. That "something" would not involve hurting her in any of the numerous ways I'd daydreamed about hurting her. I would talk to Mrs. McCready about it. There's an anti-bullying code of conduct at Bankridge, after all. However, someone needed to tell the teachers what was going on in order for them to do something about it. It looked like that someone would have to be me. I knew it might make me even more unpopular, but at that point, it was hard to imagine it was possible to *be* more unpopular.

=

"They've postponed Back-to-School Night," I said casually.

The four of us were watching a documentary about owls on TV. Enzo loves owls, especially the way they can turn their heads around to look at things behind them. He used to be convinced that he'd be able to do the same if he tried hard enough. He ended up having to see the doctor because of a neck strain.

I was sitting between the moms on the sofa, while

Enzo sat on the floor right in front of the TV. That's where he always sits if he wants to concentrate on a show. He says it's easier to remember the information if he's close to the TV. Enzo is a bit bonkers, in case you hadn't already realized. Mamma says he's "eccentric," which is just a nicer way of saying bonkers.

The moms weren't really listening to me. They seemed to be just as fascinated by the owls as Enzo was. "What was that, Liv?" Mom asked, not taking her eyes off the screen where tiny bald baby owls were squawking away in their nest.

I repeated what I'd said about Back-to-School Night.

The moms believed me. There was no reason not to. They knew that I was doing OK in all of my classes—not *amazing*, maybe, but better than I'd done in elementary school.

"Why was it postponed? And when's it going to be?"

"*Shh!* I'm trying to watch!" Enzo turned his head in a remarkably owl-like way.

Mamma hit the pause button on the remote and Enzo went to get himself a glass of orange juice.

I was ready with the answers to Mamma's questions.

I said that Mr. Lynch had been nominated for an award—the best principal in the county (*as if!*)—and the ceremony was the same night as Back-to-School Night. If he won, it would be good publicity for the school, so he thought it was a good idea to postpone Back-to-School Night. It was the best lie I could come up with, even though I had no idea if Mr. Lynch was even supposed to *be* at Back-to-School Night. I told the moms that it had been postponed for a week. I hadn't quite come up with a plan to deal with them turning up to school a week late to find it closed up for the evening. I would cross that bridge when I came to it. I had enough bridges to think about at the moment, and they were all a little wobbly to say the least.

I thought the matter was settled, so I sat back to watch some more owls in action. Then Mom said, "Why didn't they send an email? Shouldn't the school email about that kind of thing?"

I had to think on my feet (or rather, my butt). "The server was down."

I didn't even know what a server was, let alone what one being "down" actually involved. But Mom believed me! She just nodded and muttered something about technology being more hassle than it's worth.

I couldn't concentrate on the rest of the owl show, not even when it got to the gory hunting part. Part of me was relieved that the moms had believed me and that they'd be safe from the hideousness of Jade Evans. Another part of me felt guilty—*really* guilty—for lying to them.

It didn't feel right that the lies had flowed from my mouth so easily.

=

I always brush my hair before getting into bed. Gram says that when she was a girl, her mother had made her brush her hair a hundred times before bedtime. (She had to put a dollar in the Oldie Box when she told me that.) She still does the same thing every night, even though her mother isn't around to check up on her. When Gram told me that, I started doing it too. I lasted for three nights before the number of brushstrokes started to dwindle. I still force myself to do it though, even if it's only a few careless swipes. Hair as short as mine doesn't really need much brushing.

That night, after lying to my parents, I managed three brushstrokes before stopping and staring at myself in the mirror. Gram had gotten me a pale-pink dressing table with a heart-shaped mirror for my ninth birthday. It was, without a doubt, the worst present anyone had ever given me, but I told her that I loved it. I immediately set about redecorating it and now it looks pretty cool. The whole thing is covered in stickers—dinosaur stickers, space stickers, superhero stickers. Mamma says you could sell it in an art gallery. Gram never forgave me for adapting it, even though Mom tried to explain to her that I was just trying to make it a bit more "me." It's not that I actually hated pink—even though that's what I told the moms. When I was little, I used to like pink things, but that was before I realized that there were "rules." Pink things were for girls and blue things were for boys. Colors weren't just colors—they were *symbols*.

I stared at my reflection. It did not look happy.

For the first time in months, I really looked at myself. I looked hard. *What is it about me that makes them hate me so much?*

Mutant. Freak. He/She.

I tried to be objective about it, so that I could see what they saw. If I saw me walking down the street, what would I think?

It was no good. I just saw *me*. Liv Spark. Slightly awkward, uncomfortable in my own skin.

I may not have been thrilled with how I looked—especially about what was happening to my body—but I was *not* a freak.

I'm just a person. What's so wrong with that?

CHAPTER 25

Saturday was Movie Day with Mamma and Enzo. There were at least three movies I was desperate to see, but it was Enzo's turn to choose. When he came downstairs, it was clear from his outfit what kind of movie he had in mind, but I pulled him to one side and said we should let Mamma pick the movie. She'd been so down recently, with her father being so sick. I thought it might cheer her up.

I thought Mamma was going to start crying when we told her. Tears filled her eyes, but they didn't spill over. Instead, she smiled and pulled us both into a hug that was more like a headlock. "You two are just the *best*, you know?"

"But which one of us is the actual *best* best? There can only be one best." Typical Enzo.

Mamma held up her hands. "I can't call it. It's a tie. Nice try though, buddy."

Enzo opened his mouth to speak, but I got there first. "It's obviously me. Mamma just doesn't have the heart to tell you. I'm the first, original, *and* the best. You lose, shrimp."

Enzo and I ended up chasing each other around the kitchen table while Gari barked madly and Mamma laughed. Mom grabbed her car keys and headed out the front door, shouting something about peace and quiet.

Mamma chose a sucky movie about a family with two moms. *Boring*. I get why she chose it—we hardly ever get to see movies or TV shows with families like ours. But was that really a good enough reason to sit through two hours of jokes that aren't even funny, and the completely obvious family crisis that happens in the last half hour, only to be miraculously solved just in time for the super schmaltzy ending?

Mamma asked Enzo if he wanted to change before

we headed out, but he looked down at himself, smiled smugly, and said he was good to go.

"Super," said Mamma. She was used to Enzo's weirdness by now.

=

Some kids pointed, some kids laughed. I even noticed a couple of adults nudging each other and smiling. I guess they thought they were being subtle. I glared at every single one of them.

When we lined up to go into the theater, a little kid stared at Enzo in that openmouthed, completely obvious way that little kids do. It was open so wide that I could have thrown a tennis ball into his mouth. I was all ready to go over there and tell the kid's dad to teach his son some manners, but then I noticed that Enzo was smiling at the kid. The kid smiled back, so Enzo struck a pose with his hands on his hips and his chest puffed out. "Superman!" The kid squealed, and Enzo laughed and walked away.

Yup, my little brother was dressed as Superman. But

not *regular* Superman, because he doesn't actually own a Superman outfit. He was wearing his beat-up sneakers with Superman socks pulled right up to his knees. Each sock had a little red cape that flew out behind him when he ran. He also wore a pair of blue shorts, even though it was too cold for shorts, and a pair of faded red underpants worn on the outside. All of that was topped off with a Superman pajama top that was *way* too small for him and showed his belly.

Some people obviously thought he looked ridiculous, but the truth is that he didn't. He looked cool, and I'd never really thought of my little brother as cool before. It wasn't so much what he was wearing, but it was the fact that he didn't care what anyone else thought. He felt good in his outfit. Even if he didn't exactly look like a superhero, he *felt* like one.

It was all I could think about while the terrible movie got progressively more terrible. I was *proud* of my little brother. He didn't mind if people pointed, laughed, or stared at him because *he* felt comfortable. He was happy. That was all that mattered to him.

Maybe I could learn something from Enzo.

It was time to take the Pants Project to the next level.

But I couldn't do it alone, and that made me nervous. It was easier to rely on myself because I could *trust* me. Still, I was pretty sure that I could trust Jacob too.

Things had been surprisingly normal between us since I'd told him about the truth about me. We'd talked about it a couple of times. He really *was* a good listener. He'd asked me some questions: But how do you *know*? Answer: I just *do*. What happens when you start getting…? (He'd paused and vaguely gestured to his chest while looking awkward.) That one was harder to answer. I wasn't ready to think about that stuff just yet.

I texted Jacob about my idea as soon as we got back from the movie theater. He answered immediately: Sounds epic. Count me in.

And then another message a couple of seconds later: WHEN?

I thought about it before replying: **Not sure yet. Do you think Miguel and the guys would help out?**

Jacob said he would check. Mamma, Enzo, and I

were nearly home by the time his reply came through:

AFFIRMATIVE, CAPTAIN.

You know caps lock makes it look like you're shouting, right? ;)

Jacob's reply to that was a series of emojis that I couldn't even begin to understand.

Now all I had to do was work out when to put the plan into action.

CHAPTER 26

"I can't wait to see Lynch's face!" said Miguel during recess on Monday. "You know that wormy vein on his forehead? Have you guys noticed it stands out when he's angry? This could make it *explode*!"

This started a debate about whether it was possible for a vein to explode, and just how messy it would be if it actually happened.

Sav was the only one to mention that we might get in trouble, but he didn't seem all that bothered at the prospect. He'd been in the principal's office at least three times already this semester.

Jacob asked about the petition and whether it was still worth chasing signatures.

"Nah," I said, "I think the petition is dead in the water."

"This will be way more fun than a petition," said Miguel. "*Direct* action," he said, knowingly.

"So when are we doing it?" Jacob asked.

"Maybe next week? Or the week after?"

"Why wait?"

It was a good question. I was scared, I guess. Not that I'd ever have admitted it to the boys. This was my last shot. If this didn't work, nothing would. I'd be stuck wearing a skirt until high school. I couldn't bear thinking about that. For now, at least there was still the hope that my plan might change Lynch's mind. But what if it didn't work? How would I cope once the hope was gone?

=

"It's kind of tragic when you think about it," Jade said. I was unlucky enough to be standing in line right behind her. The line was always really long on taco days. Jacob and the boys were already sitting down, munching away.

"What's tragic?" asked Maisie after a few seconds.

"*Her.*"

So she wasn't talking about me for once. Jade would never use that word to describe me. I unclenched my jaw and tried to focus on the most important decision of the day: chicken or beef.

"Don't you think it's sad that Mousey Meltzer has *no* friends. Like, not even a single one?"

I craned my neck to see over Jade's shoulder. Just as I suspected, Marion was standing in line in front of her. She hadn't turned around, but she'd definitely heard Jade. I could tell from the tension in her shoulders.

"I mean, even the *mutant* has miraculously found at least a couple of people to have lunch with."

Jade must have clocked me standing behind her. Why be mean to one person when you can be mean to two at the same time? I said nothing and stared at my empty tray. I didn't hear Maisie laugh, but that didn't mean that she hadn't.

I thought Jade was going to leave it there, but a couple of minutes later she said, "Seriously, though, Meltzer, I don't think I've ever seen someone so pathetic in my entire life. How does it feel to be even less popular than the *mutant*?"

Marion still didn't turn around. A lunch server handed her a plate with three tacos on it and she walked away.

Jade wasn't happy about that because she likes to get a reaction, which is probably why she turned around to look at me.

"Can I help you, freak?"

I turned to face the lunch server. "Beef, please."

"Hey! I'm talking to you."

"How are you today?" I asked the lunch server. She was my favorite. She always gave me extra.

I could feel Jade's icy stare as I chatted with the lunch server. After thirty seconds or so, she walked away.

Who knew that ignoring someone could feel so good?

After I got my fruit and water, I headed toward the table where Jacob and the boys were sitting, but then I stopped and turned around.

Marion was sitting alone at the table in the corner. Jade, Chelsea, and Maisie were on their way to the popular table. That was just the way things were, and the way things would stay. Unless…

I veered away from the boys' table and walked past Jade's chair. I may or may not have ever so slightly nudged her with my elbow as I passed. She may or may not have spilled her soda as a result. (OK, I did, and she did.)

I walked straight over to Marion and sat down opposite her.

She didn't look up. I watched as she tore off tiny pieces of tortilla and put them in her mouth. It didn't seem to be a particularly efficient way to eat a soft taco. In fact, there was something mouse-like about it, but I wasn't about to say *that*.

"Do you think they have tacos on Mondays to try to make Mondays less terrible?" It was the first thing that popped into my head. I took a huge bite of my taco. I like to finish a taco in three bites, if possible.

"Excuse me?" She looked up.

I did that weird hand gesture that you do when your mouth is full and you want to say something—a lame sort of half wave.

I repeated myself when I'd finally swallowed my mammoth mouthful.

Marion shrugged. "I hate tacos."

"Okaaay."

"Why are you sitting here, anyway?" There was a challenge in her voice and a hardness in her eyes that I'd never seen before today.

"Felt like a change of scene." She wasn't impressed by that answer, so I tried another. "Jade is stupid. You should ignore her."

"I do. Maybe you should listen to your own advice."

Ouch. I didn't know what to say, so I focused on eating.

"If you're doing this for Jade's benefit, I'd really rather you didn't." I looked over to see Jade turned around in her chair, watching us.

"I wouldn't do anything for that girl's benefit if we were in the middle of a zombie apocalypse and she was the last non-zombified person within a hundred miles. I'd probably let myself become a zombie just to so I could go after her." I thought some more. "Although the thought of eating Jade's brain is kind of disgusting."

Marion stared at me. Maybe she wasn't used to talking about zombies. Maybe she just wasn't used to talking. But then a small smile appeared on her face. "I don't think her brain would have much nutritional value."

I laughed. A lot. Then Marion laughed too. I glanced over at Jade again, which set me off laughing again. Jade was glaring at us, but we just kept laughing and laughing. It didn't help matters that Marion's laugh itself was hilarious. There was a sort of snort right in the middle that totally cracked me up.

Marion told me she has a backpack under her bed, packed and ready just in case the zombie apocalypse actually happens.

I shook my head, smiling. "I had no idea you were into zombies."

"Why would you? You've barely said two words to me before now."

I looked down at my food. Suddenly my appetite for tacos—or anything for that matter—had disappeared. I felt ashamed. I'd been so busy feeling sorry for myself for having to wear a skirt and for being bullied, that I'd completely ignored the fact that maybe other people weren't having the best time either. I'd actually been glad that Jade occasionally gave me a break to target Marion instead. How despicable was *that*? I never thought I was that kind of person. It definitely wasn't the person I *wanted* to be.

"I'm sorry."

"For what?"

"Being like the others." It felt like the right answer. The true answer.

Marion smiled, which had to be a good sign. "How's that petition of yours going anyway?"

"Yeah, it's…not going so well, actually."

Marion raised her eyebrows. I could tell she was just dying to say something about the fact that I'd refused her help, but she was nice enough to keep her mouth shut.

Before I could answer, a figure loomed over us. "What's up?" Jacob sat down next to Marion, as if it was the most natural thing in the world.

"Not much," said Marion, "I was just asking Liv

about the pants petition." She didn't seem to think it was weird for Jacob to join us like that. And she didn't seem in the least bit shy about talking to him, which was another surprise.

I made a decision right then—one I should have made back when Marion asked me if I wanted help in the first place. It was cool that the boys were helping with the final part of the Pants Project, but wouldn't it be even better to add a girl into the mix? So I told Marion the plan and asked if she was interested in helping out. Her eyes lit up and she nodded slowly.

"I like it. A lot."

Jacob and I high-fived each other, then Marion.

"So when are we doing it?" And just like that, she was in.

CHAPTER 27

It was a good thing that I did get Marion involved. Jacob and I were debating the merits of various days to launch the plan. He thought a Friday would be best, whereas I was leaning toward a Monday, but Marion said we were both wrong. She said we should do it the day before Back-to-School Night.

"But that's in two days!" I said.

"So?"

"I need to…we need to…I don't know…"

"If we do it before Back-to-School Night, then parents can put more pressure on the teachers when they come to the school. I know *my* mom thinks the uniform policy is ridiculous, and I bet your moms do too." I didn't mention that my moms wouldn't even be at Back-to-School Night. "The key is making sure that word gets around. You need momentum."

It made sense. If pressure came from parents as well as students, surely Mr. Lynch wouldn't have a choice? We needed to make this thing a big deal—something he couldn't possibly ignore.

That's when it came to me. "Got it!" I thumped my fist on the table, which made Marion and Jacob jump.

"Got what?" Jacob asked.

I smiled secretively. "What's your dad up to on Wednesday?"

Jacob looked baffled. "What's my dad got to do with anything?"

I waited.

"*Oh*," said Jacob eventually. "I get it. You *are* some kind of evil genius. I knew it!"

"But I use my genius as a force for good!" I laughed.

"Thank goodness for that. Just make sure you don't fall into a vat of radioactive goop, OK? The last thing the world needs is a supervillain like you."

The three of us spent the rest of lunchtime trying to decide which superpowers were the coolest. (Flying, invisibility, and mind reading, *obviously*.)

=

I had no idea how the moms were going to react when I told them about the plan, but I was going to do it anyway. I felt bad enough for lying to them about Back-to-School Night—I didn't need to add to the guilt. Besides, I'd already blown my month's allowance on comic books, so I was going to need to borrow some cash.

Gram came over for dinner, but I knew better than to mention it when she was there. She wouldn't understand, and I couldn't risk her persuading the moms that the Pants Project was a waste of time.

Dinner seemed to pass in slow motion. I swear Enzo chewed each mouthful of food twenty times before swallowing, and everyone talked too much instead of getting on with the business of eating. I finished my food in five minutes flat, and spent the next fifteen minutes hiccupping.

It was late by the time Gram went home. She'd spent ages talking to Mamma about Mamma's sick father. Gram kept trying to persuade Mamma to fly out to Italy before it was too late. Mamma nodded and listened, but I could tell she was just trying to be polite. She'd made up her mind, and nothing anyone said was going to change it.

Then Gram insisted on helping Enzo with his math homework, which was entirely unnecessary. Enzo is better at math than I am. It was as if she *knew* I was desperate for her to leave.

When Gram finally did leave, I took the casual approach to telling the moms. I just came out with it when we were cleaning up the kitchen, like it was no big deal. Mom laughed out loud. "I love it!"

Mamma took a little more convincing. Luckily (and surprisingly), Mom did all of the convincing while I just stood there. Mom was talking about equality and fighting for what you believe in, and she said she was proud of me and that she was 100 percent behind me. She was doing such a good job that I decided it was best to keep my mouth shut, just in case I ruined things.

"OK, OK! I get it! I'm proud of Liv too—you know I am, right?" Mamma turned to me and I nodded. "I just worry about you getting in trouble at Bankridge…after what happened in elementary school." She was talking about The Incident.

I was about to say that this was hardly the same as me punching someone, when Mom said, "This is hardly the same! Come on, you know how important this is to Liv. And we're still planning on talking to the principal about it, aren't we? After…" Mom winced. We all knew what she'd been about to say, but talking about Mamma's father dying wasn't exactly the best way to win this argument. Mom narrowed her eyes at Mamma. "Anyway, you weren't exactly an angel at school, were you?"

I really, really wanted to know what Mom was talking about, but now wasn't the time. Mamma could go either way now, and one wrong word could spoil everything.

Mamma looked from me to Mom and back again. She was dragging it out, like a presenter revealing the winner of some reality TV show. Then she sighed. That's when I knew.

"OK!" Mamma said, with her hands up in surrender.

"Yes!" I didn't mean to shout, but I couldn't help it.

Enzo came running into the room, swiftly followed by Gari, his paws skittering across the kitchen floor. "What's happening? Are we going to Disney World?"

"Nope, it's way, way better than that," I said, giving Mamma a hug.

"I'll take you to the mall after school tomorrow," Mamma whispered while Enzo was busy quizzing Mom.

It was official: my parents were awesome.

CHAPTER 28

Marion sat with me and the boys for our strategy meeting at lunch on Tuesday. Except there wasn't actually much strategy to discuss. The plan was really very simple. Still, it was fun to write everything down and draw a completely unnecessary map. Marion even came up with a code word, but I can't tell you what it was because the information is still *classified.*

Mamma picked me up after school for our mission to the mall. We were done in less than five minutes, so she asked if we could make a quick detour for her to try on a dress she'd seen. Normally, I wouldn't be caught dead in the store we ended up in, but Mamma had done me a huge favor, so I figured I owed her this much.

While Mamma was in the fitting room, I found myself wandering over to the girls' section. I walked past rows of clothes that Jade and Chelsea would probably wear, and Maisie too, now that she'd reinvented herself.

A sales assistant asked if she could help me find anything. I said I didn't know what I was looking for, but I should have said that I wasn't looking for anything at all. I was just killing time and would have preferred to be left alone, thank you very much.

The sales assistant was about the same age as the moms, but she looked very different. She looked like she'd just stepped out of a music video. She wore a ton of makeup, but it looked good on her. Her lips were as red as a fire truck and her eye shadow looked sort of smoky. She looked me up and down with her eyes narrowed. I wanted to run away. "I've got just the thing. It's not for every day, but if you have a special occasion coming up, it would be perfect. A school dance or something?" There *was* a school dance coming up at the end of the semester, but there was no way I was going to be there.

She led me over to a rack of dresses. *Dresses!* If she'd have seen me in my normal clothes and not my school uniform, there's no way she would have thought I was interested in dresses.

She took a dress off the hanger. It was silvery, shimmery, and short. It looked like someone had skinned a mermaid.

"What do you think?" She maneuvered me over to a mirror and held it up to me. The metal bit of the hanger dug into my throat, so it felt as if she were holding me hostage.

I looked in the mirror at the dress with me behind it and the woman behind me.

If my life were a crummy movie, this might have been some kind of lightbulb moment where—*ping*—I realized that I *do* like dresses after all. Cinderella *will* go to the ball (or end-of-semester dance) and that silly "being a boy" thing was just a phase.

Instead, I took one look at myself, laughed out loud, and said, "No."

"Oh," said the sales assistant. "But it's so pretty. Don't you think?"

I tried to stop laughing, but the look on her face was too funny. You'd think I'd insulted *her* instead of some silly dress. I took a deep breath and managed to get the giggles under control. "I'm sorry."

"It's a very nice dress! It's the top seller in our Los Angeles stores."

I felt bad for her because she was only trying to help. "I'm sure it's a lovely dress. And I'm sure it would look great on someone else."

"It would look great on *you*! Go on, just try it on. I promise you won't regret it." She held out the dress to me, like it was some kind of precious offering.

I wasn't laughing anymore. "Actually, I *would* regret it. It's just not...Well, it's not *me*."

I thanked the woman, apologized for wasting her time, and walked away.

I felt different somehow. Stronger.

CHAPTER 29

Jacob's mom answered the door the next morning, smiley and bouncy. "This is all very exciting, isn't it?" she said. "And I hear you're the brains of the operation?"

I told her I liked her One Direction T-shirt, and then I almost tripped over the dog at the bottom of the stairs. He was sitting politely with his tail thumping on the wooden floor. He was small, white, and very fluffy. He didn't *look* like a Bob. He looked like he should be called Fifi Pickles or Mr. Hugglesworth. I bent down to give him a scratch behind the ears, and he flopped straight onto his back for a belly rub. Not so different from Gari after all. Looks can be deceiving. Who knows that better than me?

Jacob, Marion, and the others were in the living room. Jacob introduced me to his sister, Chloe, who was back from college for the week. She was really cool. Her clothes were all mismatched and her hair was dyed three different colors (blond, pink, and blue). She's studying chemistry (*yawn!*), but her real passion is clothes. She runs a fashion blog with one of her roommates. Chloe took a picture of us all on her phone and posted it on Twitter and Instagram. Within five minutes, she had twenty-six retweets and fifteen regrams. She was still frantically typing away on her phone when we left the house. Jacob's mom waved us off and shouted good luck as we marched down the street.

Jacob and I walked in front of the others. I told him that Enzo had been frantically practicing skateboarding to try to impress him the next time he was over for dinner. We carried on for a little while, talking about this and that, listening to Marion and Miguel be nerdy about the upcoming science fair.

We were all acting as if everything was normal. Then an old man stopped and stared at us when we were waiting to cross the road. He shook his head and muttered something under his breath when he shuffled past us. Jacob and I took one look at each other and burst out laughing.

When we got close to the school, more people started to notice. A lot more were staring, some laughing, and some cheering. A few Bankridge students started walking behind us as if we were staging some kind of protest march, which I suppose it was.

We'd timed the walk to school so that we would arrive ten minutes before the bell rang. That's when it's busiest, with hundreds of students streaming through the gates, which conveniently are located right in front of the window of Mr. Lynch's office. He likes to stand at the window and watch for latecomers. You might think he'd have better things to do, but you'd be wrong.

=

Word had got out by the time we reached the gates. There was a real crowd now. Any moment now, Mr. Lynch was bound to realize something was up—if he hadn't already. My stomach felt fizzy and jumpy, as if I'd just eaten three packs of Haribo Sour Mix.

Jacob's dad was there, leaning on the gate and sipping a cup of coffee. At least, I assumed it was Jacob's dad, since he had a huge, fancy-looking camera slung around his neck. A woman with a notepad was standing next to him, craning her neck to look at the students as they passed. A few seconds later, she spotted us and started frantically scribbling in her notepad. Jacob's dad chucked his coffee in the trashcan and started fiddling with his camera.

Jacob whispered, "Are you ready?" He held out his arm.

I linked my arm through his and said, "Let's do this."

The camera began clicking away as we walked toward the main entrance.

We stopped on the steps. That was my idea so that the name of the school would be visible in the pictures.

Jacob and Marion stood to my left, while Miguel, Alex, and Sav were on my right.

I don't think any of us had ever looked neater. Our ties were knotted tightly, our shirts were tucked in properly, and our shoes were shiny. We were everything Mr. Lynch was always droning on about during assemblies. He was adamant that every student should be "a credit to this school." We were the perfect poster students for Bankridge Middle School.

Except for one, tiny, insignificant detail.

I wore a pair of brand-new black pants. So did Marion.

Jacob, Alex, Sav, and Miguel wore skirts.

CHAPTER 30

I finally felt like me. A smarter, less scruffy version of me, but definitely me. Enzo hadn't laughed when I came down for breakfast that morning. Mom had taken a photo of me before I left the house, just as she'd done on the first day of school. I didn't mind this time, though. She took several pictures, and we looked through them together, our heads nearly touching. "You look great," Mom whispered. She sounded like she was going to cry, which was weird, but she managed to hold it together.

Jacob was wearing one of Chloe's old skirts. I had no clue where the others got theirs. Jacob had planned to wear tights too, but he'd tried them on the night before and texted me: WHAT ARE THESE THINGS?! MY LEGS FEEL LIKE THEY'RE SUFFOCATING!

I texted back: **Tell me about it.**

=

A lot of people gathered around while the photos were being taken, and most of them had their phones out and were snapping away. Some older boys were wolf-whistling and shouting things like, "Nice legs!" The boys didn't seem to mind. It did make me think, though. They didn't mind today because this was all kind of a joke, right? I mean, it was for a good cause, but people still thought it was a laugh. But what if the boys had to wear skirts every day? And what if they had to deal with girls walking behind them and shouting things about their legs or their butts. They wouldn't like it, would they? Not one little bit. And that was something girls had to go through all the time. Even so-called popular girls, like Jade and Chelsea, had to deal with boys commenting on their physical appearance. They *seemed* to like the attention—which was mostly positive—but I wondered if they really did. I hadn't given it much thought before today. The dress code wasn't just unfair to me. It was unfair to everyone.

Jacob's phone buzzed in his blazer pocket. He usually kept it in the pocket of his pants, but the skirt he was wearing didn't *have* any pockets (reason 142 why pants are automatically better than skirts). He looked at the screen and then laughed out loud. "It's Chloe," he whispered. "She says we're all over Instagram and Twitter! There's even a hashtag!"

The woman with the notepad stepped forward. "I'm Annie Lawrence from the *Gazette*. Would you like to tell me a little bit about what you're doing today?"

I'd rehearsed my little speech in front of the bathroom mirror last night. It was important to get the words just right. "We're taking a stand against Bankridge Middle School's outdated and sexist uniform pol–"

"WHAT IS GOING ON HERE?"

CHAPTER 31

We all turned around to see Mr. Lynch standing with his hands on his hips. He looked furious. His face was all red except for the tip of his pointy nose, which was bright white. The vein on his forehead seemed to be pulsating, just as we'd predicted.

Click, click, click.

I knew those pictures would be perfect. Mr. Lynch stood underneath the Bankridge Middle School sign looking like the cartoon version of an angry principal. The six of us stood a few steps below him, our backs to the camera, skirts and pants clearly visible.

Annie Lawrence took her chance. "Mr. Lynch, would you like to comment on this student protest?"

"*Protest?* This isn't a protest! It's a...it's nonsense is what it is!" He pointed a finger at us (well, mostly at me) and said, "Get inside. NOW!"

Nobody moved.

"Mr. Lynch, I presume you're aware that Bankridge is the only school in the district that forces girls to wear skirts?"

"We aren't *forcing* anyone to do anything. This is simply a matter of—" His mouth snapped shut. Unlike me, Mr. Lynch hadn't had a chance to prepare what he was going to say. He looked around to see that at least half of the crowd were holding their phones in the air, filming him. Jacob's dad was still snapping away. Mr. Lynch smiled at the journalist, but you could tell it was a fake smile. "Would you like to discuss this in my office?"

Annie smiled back, but *her* smile was genuine. "No, thank you. I'd rather discuss this right here. So, you were saying...? Girls aren't forced to wear skirts? So

Miss Spark here is perfectly within her rights to wear pants then?" I didn't like her calling me "Miss Spark," but she didn't know any better.

Mr. Lynch cleared his throat. Once, twice, three times. A bead of sweat trickled down his forehead and he wiped it away with his handkerchief.

That was when the chanting began. I don't know who did it, but it spread quickly. It wasn't particularly clever or original, but it did the job: "Pants! Pants! Pants! Pants!" Before long, it was deafening. Jacob and I stared at each other, amazed. I could see people who'd refused to sign my petition, people who'd said mean things to me in the corridor, people who'd laughed at me, and *all* of them were chanting.

Three blond figures stood at the back of the crowd, one of them standing a little apart from the other two. Maisie was chanting away with the rest of them, not even caring that Jade and Chelsea were giving her *major* evil eye.

The situation was clearly out of control. Mr. Lynch had to do something. "QUUUIIIEEET!" I don't think

I've ever heard anyone shout that loud in my entire life. I wonder if they test how loud you can shout before they let you become a principal.

The chanting stopped immediately. Obviously, everyone was having a good time pretending they cared about my campaign, but no one was willing to risk a detention for it. Mr. Lynch attempted another smile, although this one was slightly more successful. He came over and stood next to me, shuffling Jacob out of the way. "Now, as I was saying... Since Olivia came to talk to me about this issue several weeks ago, I've given it a lot of thought. Equality and fairness are issues I take extremely seriously. Of course. In fact, before I was, er, interrupted, I was just in the middle of typing up the agenda for the next PTA meeting."

"Are you saying the uniform policy is going to change, Mr. Lynch?"

Mr. Lynch held up his hands. "I'm not making any promises. It will go to a vote at the meeting a week from Thursday. But I think we can safely say that we might indeed be looking at a positive outcome for all concerned."

Everyone cheered. I didn't. What did that even *mean*? He was probably lying. He just didn't want to look like an idiot in front of the journalist. I bet he was terrified of being on the front page of the *Gazette*, looking like a fool with his angry, sweaty face.

Mr. Lynch put his hand on my shoulder. "I'd like to thank Olivia and her young friends for, um, highlighting what is clearly an important issue. When I took the position as principal of Bankridge Middle School, I made it my mission to..." He went on and on and on.

The crowd started drifting away from the front steps. Nobody wanted to listen to this garbage. It was bad enough having to put up with it in assembly.

We had to pose for a photo with Mr. Lynch, with him standing in the middle and smiling as if he'd arranged the whole thing. I could tell Jacob's dad thought it was ridiculous, but he snapped a few photos anyway, just to keep Mr. Lynch quiet.

"We did it," Jacob said under his breath, when Mr. Lynch was busy talking to Annie. "We *actually* did it!"

I shrugged. "We haven't done anything yet. The PTA might vote against it."

"Not a chance. Not once they see the article in tomorrow's paper. I bet it's all anyone will be talking about at Back-to-School Night tomorrow night. How did you know Lynch was going to back down like that?"

I didn't know what to say because I *hadn't* known. And I certainly hadn't anticipated Mr. Lynch pretending that he'd listened to me in the first place.

It felt strange because no one knew the truth about *why* I'd campaigned so hard for girls to be able to wear pants. It didn't matter, though, because I truly believed that everyone should be able to wear whatever they wanted. Boys should be allowed to wear skirts too—why not? People should be able to wear clothes that express who they are.

Of course, there was no getting past the fact that we all had to wear a school uniform. The most important thing was that it looked like we might have won. It may just be a small step in a bigger battle, but it was *something* at least. Before you know it, lots of small steps can cover a lot of ground.

=

I'd half-expected one of the teachers to tell us to go home and change our clothes, but no one did. Jacob, Marion, and I were the last ones entering homeroom, but Mrs. McCready didn't say a word about us being late. She actually winked at me as I walked past her desk.

Jacob made a big show of smoothing down his skirt before he sat down. "You know, I think I could get used to this after all. It's kind of...*airy*." He grinned.

"Why don't you talk to Mr. Lynch about making sure the change in the uniform policy works both ways?"

"Hmm, maybe we'd better leave that particular battle until next year. One step at a time." It was as if he'd read my mind!

As we left homeroom, I overheard Jade talking about how Scottish men in kilts are really hot. Chelsea agreed, nodding as fast as she could. Maisie was still sitting at her desk with her nose in a book. I wondered if Jade had dumped her because she joined in with the chanting outside. I wasn't sure how I felt about that.

=

The six of us walked into the cafeteria together. We'd stuck together at recess too—strength in numbers. By then, the boys were fed up with other boys lifting their skirts up and laughing.

None of us were ready for what happened next.

A strange silence descended upon the room as soon as the door closed behind us. Everyone, and I mean *everyone*, was looking at us. I hadn't minded the stares earlier, but now it just felt awkward.

It began with a bunch of eighth-graders over by the window. They started clapping. The clapping spread, just like the chanting in the morning. Everyone joined in, even the lunch servers. We just stood there, not quite knowing what to do. Marion blushed as red as ketchup, and Sav awkwardly shuffled his feet.

Eventually Jacob gave me a gentle shove so that I was standing in front of the others. "That's for you, Liv. Enjoy it."

And the weirdest thing was the clapping actually got louder when I stepped forward. People were clapping for *me*!

Jacob grabbed my arm and held it up high, as if I'd just won a boxing match. "Stop it!" I tried to wriggle out of his grasp.

"No chance!" He smiled. "You've earned this!"

I shook my head. "We did it together. All of us."

"Well, yeah, but someone had to be the brains of this little outfit. After all, I brought the legs to the party." He did a little twirl and gestured to his slightly knobby-looking knees.

I looked at him. His messy hair, his bright blue eyes shining with excitement. At that moment, I realized something amazing, or amazing to *me*, at least. The Pants Project meant a lot to me, and I was beyond thrilled that it actually might have worked. I was ecstatic that I might not have to wear a skirt to school for much longer. And it was nice (weird, but nice) that people were suddenly acting like I was some kind of hero. But the most important thing was that this had all happened with Jacob Arbuckle by my side. He'd stood by me through everything, even though we'd only known each other for a couple of months. He hadn't even blinked when I'd told him my secret.

I'd somehow found myself a new best friend without even trying, and that's what made me grin from ear to ear as the Bankridge students continued to clap.

CHAPTER 32

I should have known something was wrong the second I saw Mom's car outside the school gate. Jacob and I had been planning to swing by Monty's to tell the moms all about the protest.

"You didn't need to give us a ride, Mom! We could have walked. You are not going to believe what… Mom? What's wrong?"

Mom leaned out the car window and told Jacob that it would be best if he just went home. I started to say something, but Jacob was cool about it. "No worries at all. I'll see you tomorrow, Liv." He turned to walk away but not before mouthing the words, "Text me."

I got into the car and slammed the door a little too hard. "Well, that was rude. And you haven't even asked how it went today." I crossed my arms over my chest.

Mom switched off the radio and turned to face me. "Sweetie, your grandfather died. I'm sorry."

It was the strangest thing. For the tiniest millisecond, I thought she was talking about Granddad, and I felt this sharp sadness stab right through my chest, which was confusing because he had died years ago. Then she said that Mamma was already on a plane, and I finally understood.

"How's Mamma?" I asked.

Instead of answering, Mom shook her head.

We drove across town to pick up Enzo from his karate lesson. He took the news better than I did, and asked the same question about Mamma.

This time, Mom answered. "She's sad. Sadder than she thought she would be, I think."

Mom didn't ask about the protest until we got home, but I understood. We sat down at the kitchen table with a cup of tea and a plate of cookies and I told her about it, briefly. She smiled and said she wished she could have seen the look on Mr. Lynch's face.

"So can you wear pants tomorrow?"

I shook my head. "I don't think so. But maybe after the meeting."

"Are you OK with that?"

"I've waited this long. I can manage another week or two."

Mom sat back in her chair. "It's such a shame that they postponed Back-to-School Night." I nearly choked on my cookie. "We could have had a word with Mr. Lynch, see if we could help hurry things along a little. Mind you, maybe it's for the best. Mamma would hate to miss it."

"When do you think she'll be back?" I wanted to keep the conversation as far away from Back-to-School Night as possible.

"I don't know. The funeral will be tomorrow. I don't think she'll stay long after that. It depends on how it goes with her family, I guess."

I was shocked that the funeral was so soon, but Mom explained that that's how it works in Italy.

While Enzo helped Mom get dinner ready, I went upstairs and text messaged Jacob. He replied right away: I'm sorry. Death sucks. That made me smile. We texted back and forth a few times, and I explained that I'd never even met Mamma's father, but I still felt sad, so it was all a bit weird.

It was a quiet evening. We ate our dinner in front of the TV and then watched a movie. None of us really felt like talking.

=

Mamma called really early the next morning, just before the funeral. Enzo and I both had a chance to speak to her. Enzo asked if she could bring him back an Italian soccer jersey, and I grabbed the phone out of his hand before he could say anything even more insensitive. Mamma didn't want to talk about her family or how she was feeling. She just wanted to know about the protest. Even halfway across the world while going through something horrible, we were still her priority. She told me she would try to get the jersey for Enzo if they sold them at the airport, and asked if I would like one too. I said no, even though the answer was obviously yes. She said she would be home as soon as she could, and that she couldn't wait to give me a hug.

I felt extra guilty when I told Mom that I was going to Jacob's for dinner that night, and then even more guilty when she offered to pick me up. I couldn't meet her eye when I said that she didn't need to bother because Jacob's mom or dad would bring me home by nine o'clock. The truth was I would be walking back from school after Back-to-School Night. I realized I hadn't really thought through this part of the plan. What if Mom looked out the window and saw me walking up to the house? I guess I could always say they dropped me off at the end of our street. Why did lying have to be so difficult? It was never just one lie, was it? You always had to add another and another, just so you wouldn't be found out for the first one.

=

It was weird going back to Bankridge that morning. It felt as if nothing had changed, that yesterday had been a dream. I was wearing a skirt, for one thing, and nobody clapped or cheered when I walked past. The excitement was well and truly over.

When I got to homeroom, things *were* slightly different, though. Marion was sitting on a desk, talking to Todd Staveley and Kesha Lyons. She waved at me and then went right back to her conversation.

Jade didn't say anything when she walked past my desk. We did make eye contact. She rolled her eyes a little, but didn't "accidentally on purpose" barge into my chair, which she'd been doing every single day for the past few weeks.

Jacob wasn't there by the time the bell rang, and Mrs. McCready asked me if I knew where he was. I got my phone out and texted him—making sure that Mrs. McCready didn't see. She hates cell phones almost as much as she hates people who don't understand algebra. I kept checking my phone all the way through first and second periods, but there was no reply. I really hoped I wasn't going to have to face Back-to-School Night alone. I wondered if it was too late to get out of it since we didn't need to suck up to Mrs. McCready anymore.

Jacob didn't turn up until lunchtime when Marion, the boys, and I were busy reliving yesterday's triumph. The others were laughing and doing impressions of Mr. Lynch when Jacob walked into the cafeteria. Actually, he was limping rather than walking. He looked over, saw me watching, and his posture changed completely. He straightened up and tried to walk normally. When he reached our table, there was a sheen of sweat on his forehead and his face was pale.

"Hey, losers," he said as he cuffed Sav on the back of the head. He sat down heavily, and I wondered if I was the only one who noticed the relief on his face.

"Where have you been?" I asked. I wanted to ask, *What the heck is wrong with you?*

He ignored my question while rummaging in his bag and bringing out a newspaper. "This is being delivered to newsstands as we speak!" I'd completely forgotten about it! Jacob laid the paper out in front of us and there was silence as we all took it in.

The headline was huge: ***Principal Doesn't "Skirt" the Issue***. They'd gone with one of the pictures where Mr. Lynch was smiling. We all made fun of Alex, who had his eyes closed in the photo. I actually looked OK in the picture too—for once. The pants were undeniably cool.

The article was great, even though it gave Lynch more credit than he deserved. When the bell rang for the end of lunch, Jacob folded up the paper and handed it to me. "This one's yours."

I thanked him. "Are you OK?"

"I'm fine. Why wouldn't I be?" But his words were too bright and shiny. They didn't match his face. He looked exhausted.

"So where were you this morning?" I asked while on our way to class. I was deliberately walking as slowly as possible.

"I was just… I was late."

"Well, I know you were late, doofus." I smiled and elbowed him. "I'm asking *why*."

"I was...look..." He stopped in the hallway and kids streamed around on either side of us. "I was late. I'm here now. Can we just drop it?" He didn't sound annoyed—just weary. And weird.

"Sure," I said. Then I changed the subject as we walked down the hall, but my mind was racing.

Something was obviously wrong with Jacob. But *what*? And, more importantly, why didn't he want to tell me?

CHAPTER 33

We were supposed to head to the ice cream parlor a couple of blocks down from Bankridge to kill time before Back-to-School Night. But Jacob said something had come up and he'd meet me back at school fifteen minutes before Mrs. McCready had asked us to be there.

I went to the ice cream parlor alone and ordered two scoops of vanilla and one of pistachio. I liked how the colors swirled together in the bowl.

The ice cream did nothing to soothe my stomach, which felt all knotted, like a snake trying to play Twister. I couldn't stop picturing Mamma at the funeral for a man I'd never met, in a country I'd never visited. I got out my phone and sent her a quick message: **Hope you're OK. xx**

And then I freaked out a little because Mamma always forgets to put her phone in silent mode, and it would be the worst thing ever if her phone made that dumb chirruping sound right in the middle of the funeral. Then I remembered that it would be late at night in Italy, so I didn't need to worry. Not about *that* anyway.

I got a reply from Mamma a few minutes later: Thanks, topolino. I'll be fine as soon as I'm home with my famiglia. xxx

My stomach got even twistier. Why did my family have to be so nice when I was busy deceiving them?

I tried reminding myself that my motives were good. I was doing the moms a favor. Usually I can convince myself of almost anything, but as I sat there watching my ice cream melt into a pale green puddle, I knew that I was in the wrong. There was no point dwelling on it, though. Mamma was in Italy and Mom was at home with Enzo. It was too late now.

=

There were teachers milling around, getting their classrooms ready for the parents, but otherwise it was empty. I wouldn't mind Bankridge so much if it stayed like that. A whole school just for me. Then it wouldn't matter which changing rooms I used.

I waited for Jacob in the empty science lab, sitting on my usual stool at the back. He was late again.

When he finally walked in, I could tell right away that he was walking better than he had been earlier. His face was back to normal too. It was no longer pinched and pale.

"You look weird," I said.

"*Thanks*," he said sarcastically.

"What's with the hair?"

"Don't you like it?" He smoothed it down with his hand, even though it definitely didn't need any more smoothing. If you looked up the word "dorky" in the dictionary, you would see a picture of Jacob's hair on Back-to-School Night.

"Nope."

He smiled and said, "Me neither, but I'm trying to look respectable. Mom thought it might be a good idea, after yesterday. As if me looking like a total nerd will make the teachers forgive me."

"I think most of them are on our side, you know. The only one we have to worry about is Mr. Lynch."

"Who happens to be the most powerful person in the entire school," Jacob pointed out.

"Who is not going to be fooled into liking you again just because you've combed your hair. Is he even here tonight anyway?"

"I have no idea. He's probably driving around town, buying every single copy of the *Gazette* he can get his hands on."

"He'll probably use them to wallpaper his bedroom."

Jacob laughed. "He should be thanking us, really. We made him famous."

"I dare you to say that to him the next time you see him."

So, of course, he double-dared me, then I triple-dared him, and it went on and on until we decided we'd get

Sav to do it. That kid hadn't turned down a dare in his entire life.

Jacob checked his watch. "What time is your mom getting here? I told my parents to come a few minutes early so they could meet her."

"Why did you do *that*?"

"Um, my mom said she'd like to meet her. What's so wrong with that?"

I closed my eyes and tried to think. I was going to have to tell him.

"Liv?" He knew something was up. I could see it in his eyes.

I slumped in my chair. "She's not coming."

"What do you mean she's not coming? Wait, did she go to Italy for the funeral too?"

I could have lied to him right then. He'd given me the perfect opportunity by coming up with the perfect lie for me to serve up, but I couldn't do it. Not to him. I took a deep breath and told him the truth. The weird thing was that it was actually harder than telling him about me being a boy.

He didn't say anything for a moment or two. I half hoped that maybe he would call me a genius again, or at the very least say that he understood why I'd lied to my parents. When he finally looked up at me, I knew he was going to do neither of those things.

"I can't believe you did that." His voice was flat, stripped bare of any feeling.

"I suppose you'd be totally fine with your parents being laughed at by Jade Evans?" I felt it in my stomach first. The anger. Like a fire had been lit. If I wasn't careful, the flames would get out of control.

"I wouldn't care! And they wouldn't care either. Who gives a monkey's butt what Jade Evans thinks anyway?"

My jaw clenched and my hands tightened into fists. "Stop shouting at me!"

"I wasn't shouting. I was just talking loudly! And stop changing the subject. You do realize how stupid you've been, don't you?"

I wanted to hurt him right then. I hate being called stupid. Call me anything you like, but don't ever, ever call me stupid. “Shut up! It’s none of your business anyway! It has nothing to do with you!”

“What’s that supposed to mean? We’re friends, aren’t we?”

“If you were my friend, you’d understand why I don’t want my mom to come tonight.”

“I do understand, Liv.”

The flames exploded. “You *don’t*! You have no idea what it’s like! No one’s going to laugh and stare and point at your parents when they walk in! *YOUR* PARENTS ARE NORMAL!”

CHAPTER 34

The words seemed to bounce off the walls of the science lab and hit me right in the face.

I couldn't believe I'd said that.

I didn't mean it. I *didn't.*

"I..." I stopped. The words wouldn't come.

Jacob looked as shocked as I felt. "Your moms are amazing," he said quietly.

"I know," I whispered.

"They're probably the most normal people I've ever met. In a good way, obviously. It's not like they're not boring or anything."

I felt wretched. The moms would never know what

I'd said, but that didn't matter. *I* knew. The words were out there. I couldn't take them back. I couldn't *un*say them. I tried and failed to blink away the tears.

Jacob put his hand on my shoulder. "I *do* understand. Sort of. At least, I think I do. But friends also tell each other the truth, don't they?"

I saw a chance then—to deflect attention from me. "*Do* they?"

"Of course," said Jacob, looking confused.

"Then why didn't you tell me why you were late this morning? And why did you bail on me this afternoon? That's not exactly the sort of thing that *friends* do, is it?"

A bunch of emotions flitted across his face in a matter of seconds. First, he looked shocked, then angry, then sad, and then tired.

His shoulders slumped and he sighed. "You're right. I'm sorry."

That took the wind out of my sails. "What's wrong, Jacob? You know you can tell me, right?"

He took a deep breath. "I have this…condition." I

waited, nodding in what I hoped was an encouraging way. "It's called hypermobility."

"That sounds like something Superman would have," I said, trying to lighten the mood.

"I *wish*. It means my joints are really flexible—way too flexible. I dislocate my shoulder a couple of times a year, and my hip pops out of place at least once a week. And I have trouble with my ankles, and my wrists and, well, my whole body, pretty much."

"So this morning...?"

"I fell, on the way to school. My ankle just gave out." He shrugged. "It happens."

"That really sucks."

"I ripped a hole in my pants and had to go back home and change. And of course, Mom had to make a big deal about it, going on and on about how I should have used my walking stick."

"You have a walking stick?" I didn't mean to sound shocked, but the thought of someone my age having a walking stick *did* shock me. "Wait, that time you came into Monty's...that was *your* walking stick?"

Jacob nodded, then reached into his bag and pulled it out. "I hardly ever use it. It just gives me a bit more stability when the pain's bad."

"You weren't using it this morning, were you? When you fell."

He shook his head. "You know what the kids here are like. The kind of things they'd say."

Little things were starting to make sense. My brain was finally connecting the dots. "So that time you had the wrist brace? That was because of your hypermobility, wasn't it? It wasn't a skateboarding injury."

"I'm sorry I lied."

"Do you even *go* skateboarding?"

"Of course I do!" he said, indignantly. "Mom *hates* it, but she still lets me do it. She knows I just want to have a regular life. Anyway, it's no big deal. Just something I have to live with, you know? But it's no one else's business."

"So you hide it from everyone?" Then I realized something. "Just like I wanted to hide my moms," I said quietly.

He nodded and half-smiled. "Yeah, I guess so."

Suddenly everything was clear. I stood up. "But neither of us has anything to be ashamed of. Why should we hide who we are? We're freaking awesome!"

"Speak for yourself. I can't even walk down the street without falling over."

"So what? You're an *amazing* artist, you know almost as much about comic books as I do, you're brave—or stupid—enough to skateboard even though there's a good chance you'll break yourself, and…and people actually *like* you!"

Jacob blushed.

"You're a pretty good friend too," I added quietly.

"So are you."

"Thanks," I said, probably blushing too. It's way easier to give compliments than to take them.

I checked my watch. "OK, we don't have much time."

"Time for what?"

I handed him his walking stick and pulled my cell phone out of my bag.

"Showing them we're not ashamed."

"Who's 'them'?"

"Everyone," I said simply.

Jacob didn't look quite convinced.

"Come on. We can do this. We *have* to do this," I said, even though I felt sick with nerves.

Jacob stared at his stick for a second or two before slowly unfolding it.

My hand was sweaty as I dialed home.

=

It wasn't the most fun phone call I'd ever had. I jumped straight in with the truth before Mom could say anything. I told her I'd lied about Back-to-School Night, and that if she wanted to come, she had to be here in twenty minutes.

"What's going on, Liv?"

So I repeated myself and said "I'm sorry" a lot. It would have been a lot easier explaining things to Mamma.

Mom's sigh was like a big burst of static in my ear. "You know I'm in my pajamas, right? Do you want me to turn up in my pajamas?"

I said nothing.

Another sigh. "OK, I'll be there. I'll have to take Enzo to Gram's first, but I think I should be able to make it on time. And Liv?"

"Yes?"

"You'd better have a good explanation for this."

She hung up before I had a chance to speak.

=

Jacob and I were late meeting up with Mrs. McCready in the main hall. He used his walking stick to push the door open. Jade and Chelsea were already there, looking like mozzarella wouldn't melt in their mouths. Maisie turned up at the same time as Jacob and me, looking as if she'd rather be anywhere else on the planet.

Mrs. McCready glanced at Jacob's stick, but didn't say anything. The other three stared as we ran through our jobs for the evening one last time. Then Mrs. McCready sent Maisie and Chelsea to the cafeteria to fetch the coffee and tea.

Mrs. McCready handed Jade and me a pile of maps and told us to stand just inside the main entrance. “Right. Are we all sorted? Does everyone know what they’re doing?”

“Yes, ma’am,” Jade said sweetly enough to make your teeth hurt.

I just nodded.

“OK, then. Let’s get to work.” She scurried off to her classroom, leaving me and Jade—and Jacob, thankfully.

“What’s up with the stick? Is it supposed to be some kind of fashion statement?” asked Jade, but not in a mean way. She said it the same way I would have said it, like teasing a friend, because she didn’t hate Jacob liked she hated me.

Jacob smiled a confident smile. “No. I have joint hypermobility syndrome, actually.” Then he quickly turned to me and said, “Liv, why don’t you wait outside. I’ll stay here in case any early birds turn up.”

Jade was still trying to process what he’d said. Clearly, that was going to take a while. I mouthed a “thanks” at Jacob, who was looking a little stunned at just how easy it had been to tell Jade about his condition.

I headed for the door. It would be better if I could explain things to Mom before she came inside, but Jade stepped in front of me. "I don't see why you should get to go AWOL and leave us to do all the work." She crossed her arms, clearly thinking that made her look more intimidating.

"Get out of my way, Jade."

"Make me," she said, with a sly look.

"I'm warning you."

"What are you going to do? *Punch* me?" She smiled triumphantly. "Maisie told us *all* about what happened at your last school. Not exactly normal, is it? Punching someone, I mean. But I suppose we can't really expect someone like you to be normal, can we?" If you pressed the mute button and just looked at her face while she talked, you'd never know that she was spewing such hatred.

Jacob hurried over and stood shoulder to shoulder with me. "Why don't you just shut your mouth, Jade?"

Maybe he would give her a good whack with his walking stick if I asked him nicely enough? I took a deep breath through my nose. "It's OK, Jacob. I can handle this."

"*Yeah*, Jacob. Let your little freak friend fight its own battles."

"Jade's right." The look on both their faces when I said that was priceless. "I can fight my own battles."

Jade wasn't sure what to say then, so for probably the first time in her life, she said nothing at all. A wise choice.

Jacob took a step back. Also a wise choice.

I turned to Jade and just looked at her for a few seconds. I stared at her. At first, she stared back defiantly, but then she looked away. That's when I knew that I'd won.

"I'm going outside now. My mom's waiting for me. In a few minutes, she's going to come inside, and if you so much as look at her the wrong way, you will regret it. And no, I'm not going to punch you. No matter what you say or do to me, I will never punch you. Even if you really, really deserve it." I waited for a response, but none came. "What I *will* do is tell Mrs. McCready. I'll tell her every single thing you've ever said and done to me. People might call me a snitch, but you know what? I don't care what people think. I never have."

Jade's mouth opened and closed like a goldfish.

Jacob whooped and hollered like he was at a basketball game. "Now *that* is what I call a *total* smackdown." He held up his hand for a high five.

It was the most satisfying high five of my life.

CHAPTER 35

I grinned at Jacob, swept past Jade, and strode out the door.

I probably would have danced my way down the front steps if I wasn't dreading having to explain myself to my very confused, very annoyed mom.

The car was just pulling into the parking lot when I got outside. Mom drives a very old, bright green sedan—probably the least cool car you could ever imagine. I love it. I don't even know why. There's something sort of friendly looking about it.

There was nothing friendly looking about Mom, but at least she wasn't in her pajamas.

"Care to tell me exactly what's going on?" Mom asked before she'd even shut the car door.

Then she saw the look on my face and pulled me into a hug. That was what broke me. If she hadn't been nice to me, there's no way I'd have cried. I certainly wasn't looking for sympathy. I think it was the relief of seeing her, more than anything, because I realized then that I *did* want my parents here, and I was sad that Mamma couldn't be here. They had as much right to be here as anyone else. Plus, there was the teeny-tiny chance that one or two of the teachers might actually say something nice about me.

After a minute or so, Mom disentangled herself from the hug. "All right, enough with the waterworks. What's the story?"

"I'm sorry. I'm sorry. I didn't mean to lie to you, but I didn't know what else to do. I knew it was wrong, but there's this girl, and it's been really awful and I know I should have told you sooner and…and…and…"

You get the picture, right? I don't need to fill you in on everything I said. I didn't leave anything out, either.

I told her the things Jade had been saying to me, and about me. About the graffiti on my desk and the abuse hurled at me in the corridors and in the locker room. I admitted that I'd lied to her and Mamma about how bad things were.

By the time I was finished, Mom was looking really, really mad. "Who is this girl anyway? This *Jade* character. And why didn't you tell us it was so serious? Or a teacher! Why didn't you tell a teacher?"

I shrugged, and Mom took a deep breath. "I'm sorry, sweetie. I'm sorry this has been happening to you, and I'm sorry we didn't realize sooner."

I gave her the lowdown about Jade, and the fact that she was waiting inside. Mom got a glint in her eye right then. "This is going to be fun," she said.

I thought that Mom's idea of fun must be very different from mine, but the weird thing was, she was right. I don't think I'll ever be able to—or want to—forget the look on Jade's face when Mom walked right up to her, plucked a map from the pile, and said, "Jade! It's such a pleasure to meet you. Liv's told me *all* about you."

Jade looked as if she wanted to disappear. She looked genuinely scared because whatever she'd been expecting, it definitely wasn't that. Mom let go of my arm, hooked her arm through Jade's, and said, "Would you mind if we have a little chat over here? I've been *dying* to meet you!"

Jade couldn't exactly say no, and Mom didn't really give her a chance anyway. Mom led Jade off to one side while I scurried over to Jacob. He raised his eyebrows at me, a silent inquiry asking if everything was OK. I wiggled mine back and shrugged, which meant, "I have no idea."

Jacob's gaze drifted over my shoulder. "My folks are here."

I hadn't really noticed how tall Jacob's dad was at the protest, but he's huge! He looked even taller walking next to Jacob's mom, who is a very, very short person. The two of them looked awesomely odd together.

Jacob's mom's eyes widened when she saw the walking stick. She opened her mouth to say something, but her husband nudged her gently on the arm. She kept her mouth shut and gave Jacob's arm a quick squeeze.

We chatted about the pants protest, and I thanked Mr. Arbuckle for helping us out. I'd forgotten to do that yesterday, but he didn't seem to mind.

I kept glancing nervously over at Mom and Jade, but Mom had her back to me, so I couldn't see what was going on.

A couple of minutes later, Jade was back at her station next to the main entrance and Mom was walking toward us with a great big smile on her face.

"What did you say to her?" asked Jacob.

Mom just kept smiling and said, "Now *that* would be telling."

=

I never did find out what she said to Jade that night. At first, I couldn't stand not knowing. But it soon became clear that Mom was never, ever going to tell, so there was no point worrying about it. I bet she told Mamma, but Mamma would never tell me either. Those two can be infuriating sometimes. In a good way, I mean.

Jacob introduced Mom to his folks, and it turned out that they knew a bunch of the same people. I would have been happy to stay there and listen to them chat, but out of the corner of my eye, I noticed Mrs. McCready glaring at me from down the hall.

When I went back to my post next to Jade, she said something that shocked me more than any of the awful things she'd said to me.

"I'm sorry."

"For what?"

She looked down at her feet and then back up at me. "All of it."

Before I could say anything, the door opened and a steady stream of parents started to arrive. It was just as well because I didn't know what to say to Jade. A better person than me might have said, "It's OK," or, "I forgive you," but it wasn't OK and I didn't forgive her. She had made my life miserable and gone out of her way to be as horrible as possible, as often as possible. Saying sorry didn't magically fix that. It didn't magically fix *me*.

But it was a start.

=

The rest of Back-to-School Night was fine. Jade and I didn't say another word to each other. Mom managed to be polite to Maisie when she served the coffee, acting as if it was perfectly normal that they hadn't seen each other for weeks, even though Maisie used to practically live at our place. I could tell Maisie felt awkward, though, because her hands shook as she handed over the cup. Some coffee sloshed onto the floor and a teacher made Chelsea clean it up. The look that Chelsea gave Maisie was pure poison.

Mrs. McCready said some nice things about me. Apparently, it's "an absolute pleasure to teach me," which was a bit of a shock. Mom said she thought Mrs. McCready was definitely secretly impressed with the way I'd handled the Pants Project.

Mr. Eccles said that I'm one of his favorite students, even though he's not supposed to have favorites. He mentioned the incident at the start of the semester when "one or two students teased Liv a little because of her, um, your family situation," but he said that everything seemed to have been fine since then. Mom was super annoyed that he hadn't bothered asking me if things actually *were* fine. She didn't say anything to him, though. I'd asked her not to say anything to any of the teachers. There was no need. I hoped.

CHAPTER 36

The sliding doors opened and the first person who walked through was a man in a blue suit, carrying a briefcase. His eyes scanned the crowd and settled on another man in a suit, holding up a sign saying "Mr. Nakamura." Next through the doors was a family: mom, dad, and a baby. The baby spat out its pacifier, which landed on the floor and rolled toward me. I picked it up and handed it to the dad.

Mamma was the fourth person through the doors. She kept her eyes on the floor in front of her, not even bothering to look up. I whistled. (I have a very loud whistle.) Her head snapped up and looked straight at us. Then she ran.

The four of us piled into a hug: Mamma, Mom, Enzo, and me.

"What are you guys doing here?" Mamma laughed through her tears.

"You didn't seriously think we'd let you take a cab, did you?" said Mom, rolling her eyes.

"But you said it was too late to come pick me up!"

"That was my idea," said Enzo, looking supremely pleased with himself. "I thought it would be cool to surprise you."

Mamma checked her watch. "And I suppose it had nothing to do with the fact that you get to stay up three hours past your bedtime?"

"Busted!" I laughed.

"Straight to bed the second we get home, OK?" said Mamma. Then she saw Enzo's epic pout and said, "Straight to bed *after* a cup of hot chocolate. So, what have I missed?"

"Nothing much," I said, managing to keep a straight face for approximately 2.5 seconds.

"Liv has *news*, apparently," said Mom. "But she wouldn't tell me any more until you got home."

"Well then, I think news calls for hot chocolate, so let's get out of here!"

I trailed behind them on the way to the exit. I had that jumpy, nervous feeling in my stomach again, but this time it was different. I *was* nervous, but I was excited too.

It was time. Time to tell the truth. Time to trust.

=

I'd decided that afternoon, and as soon as I had made the decision, I felt better about everything. The decision crept up on me as I watched Jacob tell Sav and Miguel about his hypermobility. He wasn't using his walking stick, so it wasn't as if he *had* to tell them. It happened at the end of lunchtime when Miguel asked if Jacob wanted to play basketball after school. Jacob said he'd love to, but he was in quite a lot of pain. When the boys asked what was up, he just came out with it. "I have this condition that affects my joints. My wrists are pretty bad today."

And that was it. The boys just accepted it. Miguel said, "Bummer," and Sav made a joke I didn't understand. Jacob did his best to act cool, but his relief was obvious.

I mentioned it on the way to class. "That wasn't so bad, was it?"

Jacob looked thoughtful. "You know, it really wasn't. It feels…good. It was starting to stress me out, you know? Making up excuses all the time, remembering which lies I'd told to which person."

"Is it really bad today? The pain, I mean?"

Jacob shrugged. "My ankles are way better than yesterday. It gets to a point where you're relieved when it's just one part of your body that hurts."

"I can't imagine what it must be like."

"I'm glad you don't have to. But seriously, I feel so much better now that I don't have to hide it."

I thought about that for a moment or two, and then he said, quietly, "You were right last night. When you said there's nothing to be ashamed of. No one should ever be ashamed of who they are."

I thought about that for more than a moment or two.

Then I thought about it through English, Spanish, and math class. Then I made up my mind. I told Jacob and he asked me if I was sure.

"I've never been so sure about anything in my life."

=

I tried to remember how sure I was when we got back from the airport just before midnight. Enzo fell asleep in the car, so Mom carried him up to bed. That left the three of us sitting at the kitchen table, each with a huge mug of hot chocolate.

I asked what it had been like for Mamma to see her family after so much time.

"I thought it was going to be awful. They…said some very hurtful things a very long time ago. Some things that are very hard to forgive."

"Like what?" I asked, out of pure nosiness.

"It doesn't matter now," said Mamma. "What matters is that I talked to *my* mamma, after the funeral. I'd wanted to leave right away, but there were no flights. Turns out that was a blessing in disguise." She took a shaky breath and smiled at Mom, who took hold of her hand. "She really wants to meet you guys. All of you."

Mamma explained that her father had always been in charge of the family. Everyone had to do things *his* way. "I hadn't actually realized how hard it was for my mother. Not that she's glad he's gone or anything. She loved him very much, but now, well, things are different now. She said she'd like to come see us next summer, if we would have her."

"That's amazing!" I said because Mamma looked really happy about that. And that meant I was happy about it too (and a little terrified of this scary Italian grandmother I'd never met).

"Enough about me, what's the big news?" asked Mamma.

Oh boy. Here goes nothing.

My voice was shaky as I said it wasn't really news, just something I thought they should know. About me. Something very important.

The moms exchanged a look and Mom said "It's OK, sweetheart, we—"

"Shh, let Liv finish," Mamma said, reaching out for Mom's hand and mine.

We stayed like that, hands clasped together, as I told them the truth.

Mamma burst into tears, just like I'd been worried she would. I sat, there horrified. I'd made a terrible, terrible mistake.

But when Mamma saw the look on my face, she laughed. "No, *topolino*! I'm crying because I'm happy!"

"Happy? Why?"

Mamma squeezed my hand. "How can we *not* be happy? All we want is for *you* to be happy, my darling. And a big part of that is accepting who you are."

"You knew, didn't you?" I didn't say that I'd overheard them talking about me that one time. There was no point.

The moms exchanged another look, which confirmed my suspicion.

"Why didn't you say anything?"

Mom put her hand on my shoulder. “We didn’t *know*. We thought it was a possibility, that’s all. But it needed to come from you first. You can understand that, can’t you?”

A horrible thought washed over me. “What about Gram? And Enzo? Do *they* know?”

“No, they don’t. We can tell them, though, if you want us to. It’s totally up to you.”

“I don’t know what… I’m not sure what I’m supposed to do now.”

Mamma stroked the back of my hand. “You don’t have to do anything. We can talk about this whenever you’re ready. There’s no rush.”

We talked a bit more, and it felt so easy and right and made me annoyed with myself for not doing it sooner. I should have known the moms would understand.

Mamma told me about a youth group at the LGBT center where she volunteers. She said there were a bunch of kids just like me, and I could go with her sometime. “No pressure,” she said. I said I’d think about it.

After a while, Mom said, “So how are you feeling now, Liv?”

“I feel…good.”

That made them both smile, but Mamma still looked a little worried. “You’re not worried or confused about anything?”

“Nope,” I grinned. “I just feel like *me*.”

CHAPTER 37

Three months later...

Happy birthday to me! Twelve years old as of 5:47 a.m.

We had Dante's red velvet cake for breakfast. It's his specialty.

Gram came over last night for a pre-birthday meal. It's always good to stretch out the celebrations for as long as possible.

It's also always better to open Gram's present early. That way you're not disappointed on the day itself.

We gathered at the kitchen table and Gram put down a big box. The wrapping paper was bright pink and the whole thing was wrapped up in a white satin bow. It looked alarmingly like the sort of boxes I used to get from her when I was little—the ones with creepy dolls inside.

"Go on then! Open it!" Gram's eyes were all twinkly with expectation.

I took a breath and readied myself to smile no matter what was inside.

I tore one tiny corner of the paper, reluctant to go any further. "Get on with it!" Enzo shouted. Gari woofed his agreement.

So I did.

And I smiled. A real smile. The realest smile you can get.

It wasn't a doll. It wasn't a pink dress. It wasn't a doll *wearing* a pink dress.

It was a skateboard. An absolutely amazing skateboard. Red and black with silver lightning bolts.

"Do you like it?" Gram asked. She seemed a bit shy all of a sudden. "I'm told it's quite a good one, but I can take it back to the shop and exchange it if you don't like it."

"No, I don't like it."

Gram's face fell and her shoulders drooped. The moms looked ready to strangle me.

"I *love* it! Thank you *so* much!" I threw my arms around her and gave her the biggest hug. "This is the best birthday ever!"

"But it's not even your birthday yet!" Gram laughed.

"I don't care! Nothing could top this!"

It turned out that Jacob had been called in as Expert Skateboard Consultant. So that's why he'd been acting weirdly excited about *my* birthday. I texted him after dinner, and he said he'd come over at the weekend to teach me the basics.

The moms told Gram about me being trans after double-checking that I was cool about it. She was still getting used to the idea, but she was trying her best. They'd told Enzo too. Apparently, he just shrugged and said, "OK," before going back to building his Lego castle. He'd always treated me like a big brother anyway, so nothing was going to change there.

Mamma's taking me to the youth group at the LGBT

center next week. I thought it would be a bunch of kids sitting in a circle, talking about their feelings, but they're having a movie night apparently. I can definitely handle a movie night. And maybe talking about my feelings wouldn't be so bad after I get to know people a little. After all, it worked out OK with Jacob, didn't it?

I've been thinking about maybe changing my name. Liv might be better than Olivia, but it's still not quite right. Enzo thinks I should go for Tony because he's obsessed with Iron Man, but I'm definitely not going to do that. I'm not going to rush into anything. It's not every day you get to choose your own name, so I need to make sure it fits exactly right, like my favorite pair of Converse.

=

A few months ago, I would have dreaded going to school on my birthday, but things are different now.

Getting dressed for school still gives me a little buzz of happiness, even after two months of wearing pants.

At least half the girls at Bankridge wear pants now. Including Jade Evans.

The PTA vote wasn't even close. Only two people voted to keep the uniform policy the same. When Mr. Lynch announced it in assembly, he acted like it was all his idea, but I didn't mind. I knew the truth and that was all that mattered. He hadn't said a word to me since that day on the steps. I'd half expected him to haul me into his office and shout at me, but he hadn't. I'm not sure why.

I'm not going to pretend that everything is wonderful all the time. It's not entirely a case of "*and they all lived happily ever after*."

But how about this instead? "*And they all lived* mostly *happily ever after…and managed to ignore the occasional idiot saying something stupid.*"

That's good enough for me.

It turned out that I was right about Maisie being dumped by Jade and Chelsea. I felt bad when I saw her moping around on her own, but then I reminded myself that *she* was the one who'd dumped *me*. Still, I was glad when she started hanging around with Vanessa Durden.

Vanessa seems to be a nice person. Maisie is too, and maybe she just forgot that for a while.

Jade and Chelsea mostly ignore me altogether, which is absolutely fine with me. There's been *some* progress though. They haven't bullied Marion since the Pants Project—not even once. And last week, Jade was one of the team captains in basketball and she picked me first to be on her team. We won; I scored fourteen of our nineteen points.

Jade likes to win. So do I.

=

I arrive early at school, but someone else has arrived even earlier. The room is empty, but there's a silver helium balloon tied to my chair and an envelope lying on my desk.

I open the envelope and look at the card inside.

The front of the card has the most amazing drawing on it. It looks professional—like something you'd find in one of my comic books.

The drawing is of two superheroes.

One of them looks like me and the other one looks like Jacob. Superhero Me is dressed in black and red to match the skateboard under my feet. Superhero Jacob is dressed in the same colors, but he's wearing a skirt. He's also carrying a walking stick, but it's a souped-up, turbo walking stick with flames shooting out of the end.

The drawing has a caption underneath it:

SUPERLIV & BENDY BOY!

I open up the card.

HAPPY BIRTHDAY, SUPERLIV!

From your friend and sidekick,

Jacob Arbuckle

I close the card and stare at the picture on the front. It is the best birthday card I've ever seen. My name doesn't seem so bad when it has "super" in front of it.

"So, are you ready for our next adventure?" I hadn't

even heard him come in. He's stealthy, this sidekick of mine. "What's our next mission?" Jacob raises his eyebrows expectantly.

I smile and do my best to look mysterious and suitably superhero-y. "Now *that* would be telling."

ACKNOWLEDGMENTS

Thank you to Julia Churchill, Hélène Ferey, Jennifer Custer, and Allison Hellegers for being entirely brilliant.

Thank you to Aubrey Poole, Annie Berger, Cassie Gutman, Alex Yeadon, and the entire team at Sourcebooks for believing in Liv's story.

Thank you to Glenn Tavennec, Fabien Le Roy, and the Robert Laffont crew for your unwavering support.

A huge thank-you to those who have shared their stories with me and those who have read and provided feedback.

Thank you, as always, to Caro Clarke for being my first and final reader (and for still laughing at my jokes even though you've read them at least ten times).

And finally, thanks to you, the reader, for picking up this book. I hope you enjoyed reading *The Pants Project* as much as I enjoyed writing it.

ABOUT THE AUTHOR

Cat Clarke is an award-winning YA author from the UK. *The Pants Project* is her debut middle-grade novel. She lives in Edinburgh, Scotland, with her partner, two ninja cats, and two decidedly non-ninja cocker spaniels.